SUMMER DREAM

Amy was shocked when her business partner disappeared with most of the money from the sale of their joint gardening venture. She decided to take up the new owner's suggestion and go to Cornwall to seek employment — someone he knew owned a studio and craft business there. When she arrived at the pretty village, Amy thought it seemed the ideal place to spend the summer, trying to put the recent unhappy events behind her. But the dream was to become a nightmare . . .

Books by Joyce Johnson
in the Linford Romance Library:

JOYCE JOHNSON

◆

SUMMER DREAM

Complete and Unabridged

LINFORD
Leicester

sou 8/04

First published in Great Britain in 1999

First Linford Edition
published 2002

British Library CIP Data

Johnson, Joyce, *1931* –
  Summer dream.—Large print ed.—
Linford romance library
1. Large type books
2. Love stories
I. Title
813.5'4 [F]

ISBN 0-7089-9864-X

Published by
F. A. Thorpe (Publishing)
Anstey, Leicestershire

Set by Words & Graphics Ltd.
Anstey, Leicestershire
Printed and bound in Great Britain by
T. J. International Ltd., Padstow, Cornwall

This book is printed on acid-free paper

1

Amy Barton, juggling shoulder bag, briefcase and shopping, practically hopped up and down on the doorstep in frustration as she twisted her key in the lock.

'Perfect end to a perfect day! The key's stuck,' she said aloud.

Bags and shopping slid out of her arms, and the key finally twisted in the lock. She pushed open the front door. Thank goodness, she could hear the TV which meant Sue was back.

Sue's hours as a tourist guide in mid-season Bath could be erratic and it was a blessing that for once her cousin had an early finish. Amy desperately needed a shoulder to cry on. She made straight for the sitting-room.

'Hi, Amy, you're back early and in time for the Centre Court match.'

Momentarily Sue Barton flicked her

eyes from the screen.

'Good day? How did the meeting . . . ah! I can see. Not good?'

'Worse than that — bad. Horrendously bad!'

About to collapse on the sofa she shot up again.

'And wouldn't you know it, I've left all my stuff on the doorstep. I expect the cats will have eaten the food, a passing thief stolen my bag, and who cares about my brief-case! Lots of horrible work.'

'Sounds like a really bad day. Take a few calming breaths then come and tell me all about it,' Sue called after her.

She didn't switch the TV off right away. It was difficult to gauge the scale of this particular crisis. Cousin Amy's life had been a series of crises ever since she could remember, 'way back to the earliest days of their shared childhood. She waited until the tennis rally ended then went into the kitchen. Amy was rummaging in the fridge.

'Coffee?' Sue offered.

'I need something stronger to counteract the shock. Have we any wine?'

'Bottom shelf, at the back. I'll get it.'

'No, I will. You're missing out on the tennis. I need to calm down a bit otherwise I'll be exploding over you.'

'The tennis doesn't matter, now when you're so upset. What's happened? You were bouncing this morning, couldn't wait to get to the accountant's to pick up the cheque. I thought we'd be celebrating tonight. Come on, Amy, the suspense is killing me. Tell!'

Amy uncorked the wine, set two glasses on the breakfast bar and filled them to the brim.

'So,' Sue said and sat down opposite her cousin, 'explain.'

'I can't explain, but I will tell, and see if you can make some sense of it. You know I had to see the accountant this afternoon?'

'Yes, to pick up the settlement cheque. That's why I thought . . . '

'Perfidious Tom!' Amy burst out.

'What?'

3

'Tom Cheat! Tom Liar! Tom Wheeler Dealer!'

'Tom Barrett? Dear old Tom? Your partner?' Sue interrupted.

'The same. Good, old, solid Tom, my ex-partner. Tom, the biggest conman in Bath, only surpassed by me, the most gullible simpleton in the UK.'

'But why?' Sue was bewildered. 'I thought the deal was signed and sealed, a watertight legal agreement. You and Tom Barrett between you agreed to sell Greenfingers to Archdale Garden Centres, price half a million pounds.'

'Correct, and very pleased we were, Tom with his ninety per cent, which was fair enough because it's his Greenfingers. He put in the original capital.'

'But it was practically a write-off until he persuaded you to work for him, and he made you a partner last year.'

'Only because I threatened to leave. I was working for peanuts, and the business was coining money.'

'And all down to you.'

4

'Not entirely, but yes, I did put a lot into it. I enjoyed it. I trusted Tom when he said to put Greenfingers on the map and it would be snapped up. We would share the proceeds. He promised me fifty thousand pounds, enough for me and you, Sue, to start our dream project, our specialised travel company.'

'So what happened? Didn't the accountant pay up?'

'Oh, yes, I got the money.'

Amy scooped her bag from the floor. 'Here it is.'

Amy pushed over the cheque and Sue looked at it in disbelief.

'But there's a zero missing. It's a mistake. This is made out for five thousand pounds, not fifty thousand.'

'True. Now do you see why I'm just a little upset?'

'It's obviously a mistake. Didn't you tell the accountant?'

'Of course I told him, but he was as baffled as I was. The amount was correct according to his instructions.'

'From whom?'

'Mr Tom Evil-Devil Barrett's solicitor, the guy I thought was acting for both of us as Greenfingers' partners, the guy brokering the deal with Archdales. You see I never for one second considered . . .'

Silence fell in the room and Amy appeared to have gone into a trance.

'And?' Sue prompted. 'The solicitor, couldn't he put it right?'

Amy's laugh was bitter.

'He could, because it was right. He had acted precisely by Tom's instructions. This is the really hard bit, Sue. I can't believe I could have been so stupid, so naïve. You know I left all the business side to Tom, just signed everything he put in front of me.'

'Without reading any of it?'

'Yes. You know how much I hate paper work of any kind, and I trusted Tom. I never had any reason to doubt him. He was, or appeared to be, such a kind, old guy, straight as an arrow, whereas he's crooked.'

'But you did all the work to build up

Greenfingers. It was nothing but a country nursery until you took it on and now it's a mega business worth half a million. How can this happen?'

'It's happened because I never checked out a thing. I trusted Tom Barrett and I believed every promise he made.'

'You can sue him. He's broken your agreement. You're a partner. He can't get away with it. Where is he?'

'Huh, no loose ends. After that wild party to celebrate at Greenfingers, Tom disappeared, left the country with his cash. I've nothing in writing, nothing that would stand up in court. And the last straw is there never was a legal partnership, just a worthless piece of paper Tom made up to keep me quiet.'

Amy ended in a rush and looked apprehensively at Sue.

'You'll hate me now — all our plans for that money. I've let you down.'

Sue's expression was unfathomable.

'I just can't believe it. You beavering away for six years and all the time old

Tom, the dozy dodderer we called him, must've been planning this all the time. It's so crazy.'

'OK, crazy maybe, but all our plans'll have to go on hold. You're stuck as a tourist guide for the duration, and I'll be working for Archdales.'

'Come on, Amy, I can survive the tourist invasion a bit longer.'

'But I know you're bored with it all and now we're both stuck in the same old rut. What shall we do?'

Sue stood up.

'Put the shopping in the fridge, have a quick wash and brush up, then we'll go out for supper, somewhere expensive. We're going to forget Old Tom, and my schedule tomorrow, and do a blessing count. We've got five thousand in the bank, both working, nice house. Forget the mortgage! We've years ahead of us to do our scheme. What's money, after all?'

Amy picked up the cheque.

'Right, let's make a tiny dent in this right now. I know a great restaurant.'

She hugged Sue.

'Thank goodness, too, for my cousin, the best friend I'll ever have.'

'It's mutual,' Sue replied.

Amy and Sue Barton had spent an idyllic childhood on a Yorkshire Dales' sheep farm jointly owned by their fathers. The Barton brothers had married local sisters and the two families lived closely-entwined lives. The enterprising sisters took aside a few acres of farmland and ran a plant centre and mail-order nursery business. Here, Amy learned the expertise Tom Barrett had found so useful. But as the cousins grew to teenagers, the charms of rural isolation palled and the two young girls planned their escape to city lights. London was their aim but a quirk of fate led them to Bath where they had now lived together for the last seven years. Both worked as tour guides until Tom Barrett had inveigled Amy into working for him.

'That was fantastic,' Amy said later,

mopping up the last of the sauce. 'Amazing pasta. Now what about dessert? Wow, look at these. Two thousand calories each at least. Just coffee for me.'

'Me, too,' Sue replied, nodding to a waiter.

'I feel so much better,' Amy said. 'Nevertheless I do think we should make a positive plan. We never intended to spend seven years in Bath.'

Sue stirred her coffee, eyes downcast.

'My fault, because of perfidious Gary, the deceiver.'

She spoke lightly but her eyes clouded with remembered pain.

'Not your fault. How were you to know he was married with two kids?' Amy commented.

'It took me long enough to find out,' Sue said ruefully.

'Rotten Gary!'

'Rotten Tom!'

The cousins spoke simultaneously, then burst out laughing. Amy lifted her glass.

'A toast to the future. We'll give it one more year. You dazzle the tourists with wonderful Bath and I'll zoom up the corporate ladder at Archdales. Then we're on our own, beg or borrow the money, remortgage the house, cajole the parents. One year,' she repeated. 'Agreed?'

'Agreed,' Sue replied, clinking her glass to Amy's.

Amy found it hard to sleep that night. Try as she might to forget the past and concentrate on the future, Tom Barrett's treachery worried and nagged at her. How could she have misjudged him so? He'd been a father figure for years and she'd loved working with him to expand Greenfingers. She had flair and imagination and was wonderful with customers.

It had been an astonishing success but Amy had always regarded it as a stepping-stone to her main goal in life — Tailormade Vacations, in partnership with Sue. She had an important meeting with one of Archdales' directors later in the morning, to discuss company strategies.

I'll have to do what they want, with my hands tied by their public limited company policies, she thought, lying awake. At least Tom Barrett had given her totally free rein, though much good it had done her! She renewed her vow to Sue before falling into an uneasy sleep.

'Just one more year and that's my limit.'

2

'Amy, there's a customer who insists on speaking with you, in Greenhouse Five. Can you come?' the voice on the phone said.

'Give me ten minutes, then I'll be there.'

Amy replaced the phone and smiled placatingly at the scowling chef.

'Problem, Eddy?'

'What else? Ever since Archdales took us over there've been nothing but problems, but this is the last straw.'

Dramatically, he threw down a paper.

'This fax orders me to buy direct from Archdales' catering suppliers, in Newcastle of all places! I refuse to use anything but local, fresh produce in this restaurant. That's what our reputation's built on.'

'I know. You've done a wonderful job.'

'If they are going to change Greenfingers beyond recognition, why take it on? Our customers come because we are us, unique, not part of some huge conglomerate.'

'You're right. There's someone coming down from Archdales today. I'll speak to him.'

'Mr Warner's here.'

As if on cue, Carol, Amy's assistant, poked her head round the door.

'Who?' Amy asked, taken unawares.

'Dan Warner, one of Archdales' big chiefs.'

'Is it that time already? Can you stall him, give him coffee?'

'I don't have the time to be stalled, Miss Barton, and we'll have coffee together to save time.'

A large, grey-haired man, immaculately and expensively-suited, gently removed Carol from the doorway and walked into the office.

'Er, Mr Warner, I'm sorry.'

Amy surreptitiously wiped her palm on her trousers. She'd been potting up

14

plants earlier and she felt grubby. She was not all at her sparkling best to meet Archdales' Resources Director, whatever that was. It sounded important, and Dan Warner looked a match for the title. Eddy fidgetted.

'Not now,' Amy said sharply, noting the belligerent gleam in the chef's eye, eager to have his say.

The Resources Director summed up the situation at a glance.

'If there's a problem, Miss Barton will tell me and I'll pass it to the appropriate department.'

Dan Warner's voice was steely, and somehow Eddy was manoeuvred across the room and out the door, his protests lost in the outer office. Two seconds later he popped back.

'I shall send over my special filter coffee and personally-baked biscuits. We are a small, specialist organisation, Mr Warner,' he burst out.

Amy groaned. Her head was spinning. She had too much to do, and had had too little sleep. Mr Warner wasn't

going to be impressed by her management skills today! She tried out an
executively dazzling smile.

'Do sit down, Mr Warner. I didn't
expect you quite so early. It's been one
of those mornings. Carol, not now.'

'The customer from Greenhouse
Five,' Carol hissed. 'He must see you.
It's Mr Deane.'

'OK, OK, I'll come. Just give me ten
minutes, Mr Warner. Coffee will be
right with you. Make yourself at home.
There's . . . er . . . gardening manuals
in that cupboard.'

'I'd prefer to see the month's
accounts. You do have a print-out?'

'Ah! I haven't quite, but will have later.'

Leaving the vague promise hanging
in the air, she fled, and it was well over
half an hour before she reappeared, full
of profuse apologies.

'That was Tony Deane, an extremely
important customer, a landscape gar-
dener who sends us lots of customers.'

She ran an agitated hand through her
hair.

'Customers are essential. No customers, no profits, no dividends for shareholders. Profit is what Archdales Garden Centres is all about, and don't worry, I've made good use of the time.'

Carol burst into the room.

'Sorry to interrupt but Jack says the leak in the sprinkler system . . . '

Dan Warner stood up.

'Let Jack see to that, and if there's anything else, you can probably deal with it. It's apparently impossible to hold a private conversation here. I'm taking Miss Barton out to lunch.'

'But I do need to see Jack. And there's a delivery expected.'

Amy was becoming more flustered.

'Someone else can surely check that,' the big man said tersely. 'Haven't you learned that one of the first principles of management is delegation? You're not supposed to do everything yourself. Your job is to manage other people, organise your staff so you're free to make the major decisions.'

'But it's the personal touch that's

made Greenfingers such a success.'

Amy took her jacket reluctantly from its hanger.

'Greenfingers is history. Archdales is the present and the future.'

Dan Warner steered a protesting Amy out to the carpark and drove off to a nearby restaurant where he acquired a table almost immediately.

Perhaps the most astute of Archdales' directors, Dan Warner studied the girl seated across the table from him. He shouldn't really have brought her out to lunch. It had been an impulse, a whim, but there was something about Amy Barton, a vivacity and zest that reminded him of his daughter, Holly, before she'd lost the will to do anything. He cleared his throat.

'Amy — I may call you Amy?'

'What else? That's me.'

She wiped her mouth.

'That was great. I didn't realise I was so hungry.'

'It's good to see.'

He leaned back.

'You're enjoying working for Archdales?' he asked.

'Of course.'

It was a stock question, so she gave it a standard response.

'You'll obviously notice the difference from working at Greenfingers, a small, private business.'

'Oh, yes, that was the greatest fun, especially at the beginning, building up, trying new ideas, taking risks, pleasing customers.'

'That's Archdales' aim, pleasing customers.'

'Sure, but through Greenfingers, I know all our customers personally. It was like a family. That's why when Tom . . . ' She stopped abruptly.

'Tom? Tom Barrett, the ex-owner?' Dan Warner inquired.

'Yes.'

'Something wrong about Mr Barrett, Amy?'

'No.'

'You sure?' he asked, then gave himself a mental shake.

It was none of his business. He had to get on with it.

'I'll come straight to the point, but perhaps coffee first?'

'Shouldn't we be moving, getting back? I've a stack of things piled up.'

Amy wondered what was the point he was taking so long in reaching.

'So I saw. We note you are a most conscientious employee. We monitor staff very closely after a take-over. There's often euphoria after a big payment, and the shelving of responsibilities, often followed by bewilderment and confusion, dislike maybe of the new order imposed by larger corporations.'

'But I didn't get a big payment and I'm not part of a family firm. I was, or thought I was, a partner.'

'Thought you were?'

'Look, Mr Warner, I don't know where this is leading. I'm probably not right for Archdales' style right now, but I can learn, go on a course, though I think things are going OK as they are.'

Dan stirred sugar into his coffee.

Amy watched. He was so long she finally asked, 'Something wrong, Mr Warner?'

'Yes. I'm sorry, but there is. I'm afraid we're viewing the situation from different perspectives. Archdales is multi-national, run on extremely precise lines, company lines. There's no room for deviation or for personal idiosyncrasies. We train our managers rigorously to respect that.'

'I've said, I'll go on your course.'

He smiled ruefully.

'You make it sound like a week's holiday. It's not like that at all. We train from the floor in every aspect of the business.'

'You're trying to tell me something. And from your expression, it's not something I want to hear. I wish you'd get to the point.'

'I will. I'm sorry, Amy, but it's not our policy to employ on-site managers. It's led to problems in the past, and we do make that clear during take-over negotiations. It shouldn't be that much of a surprise to you.'

'You're sacking me?'

'I see it is a surprise. Surely Mr Barrett . . . '

'Mr Barrett, friend and partner, chose not to tell me anything.'

'But you were a partner, involved in the discussions, surely?'

His disbelief was almost comical.

'So I thought. I've been a stupid, gullible fool and this makes it worse. Not even a job! I can't believe what a stupid fool I've been.'

'You wouldn't be the first, not by a long chalk.'

Dan's tone was grim and his heart twisted with pity, but he'd been right. Amy Burton wasn't fashioned in the business mould.

Tentatively he said, 'You must be financially secure as a partner.'

He didn't know the details. His task came after all the deal making.

'No. I got five thousand pounds, when I'd been promised fifty thousand and he's left the country. It's not the money so much as my misjudgement. I thought Tom was as straight as they come, and I thought he liked me.'

Dan hesitated. She'd been unbelievably foolish, just the way Holly would've been. He sighed.

'Look, Amy, if you really want to work for Archdales I could put you forward for training but it'd be from the bottom, a long, hard slog, and frankly I don't think you'd fit into our career structure. I know it's no business of mine but why don't you make a clean break, a fresh start? You're a girl with lots of talents.'

'Huh! Such as? And where? What as? I'm not qualified for anything.'

She wasn't going to confide in him her dream. No-one, apart from Sue and herself, knew about that, not even her parents.

'Rubbish! Look what you did with Greenfingers. Don't be so modest. Tell me what you are good at.'

'I'm a dabbler, on the fringes. I love plants, the actual nursery work,

23

planting, propagating. I've an eye for what sells, and that old cliché, I like people and am good with them. Nothing else, really, except the usual stuff, cooking, food, travel, piano and I can paint a bit. Not much of an inventory.'

'On the contrary, it's more than most people could dig up, and of course you take your best assets for granted.'

'What are those?'

'Youth, and time. Five thousand pounds is a nice little cushion, and I'll try and squeeze some severance pay. Now, this is personal. You don't need to answer but do you have a serious boy friend?'

She shook her head.

'Easy then. You break out, get in your car, spin a coin and go wherever it points.'

He took a pound coin from his pocket.

'Heads south, tails north.'

'Not north, I've done that.'

Amy felt a tremor of excitement.

'All right. Tails east, heads west.'

The coin spun, he caught it in his left palm and slapped it down on the back of his other hand.

'Royal command, the Queen's head. Go west, young woman, and that's given me an idea. There's a man I know in Cornwall, a real maverick, with lots of irons in lots of fires. Possibly he could give you some ideas.'

Amy caught her breath as excitement blossomed. Freedom from responsibility, adventure — possibilities flowered.

Dan scribbled on the back of a card.

'Here's his name, and the village. I don't know the address but it's a coastal village so you're sure to find him. He runs a studio and craft business and goodness only knows what else. You'll like him.'

Amy took the card.

'Jack Coverack. Sounds a bit like a pirate! Thank you, Mr Warner. I might do as you suggest.'

'I sincerely hope you will. And it's Dan, now the business part's over. Pity about Archdales, but it wouldn't be right for you and I've an old bones feeling you could be on the brink of a big adventure.'

'At least it'll be a holiday, and I've never been to Cornwall, would you believe?'

Impulsively, she got up and hugged him.

'Thanks, Dan. Thanks for knocking off the shackles.'

He flushed with pleased embarrassment.

'It's certainly been different from the the usual meeting.'

He glanced at his watch.

'There's not enough left of the day to go back to Archdales. Your record shows a spell as a tour guide. Why don't you show me around Bath, ending up with tea and buns at the Pump Rooms?'

'My pleasure. I hope Archdales won't want too much notice. Now the idea's in my head I can't wait to set off for Cornwall.'

'I'll do the best I can.'

26

'Change your mind and come with me.'

Amy leaned out of the car window.
Sue laughed.

'We've been through this argument.
I'm going to work out the main season
here, then we'll see. I'll join you for a
few days if and when you settle
anywhere. Anyway, it's your adventure.
You need a break to get over all the
Greenfingers' hassle.'

'I've almost forgotten all that. I'll
miss you.'

'Me, too. Now go! No point in a
crack of dawn start if you're going to
hang around in the road.'

'Right, I'm gone. See you soon.'

Amy waved until her cousin had
vanished from her rear view mirror,
then settled back to enjoy the drive. The
roads were gloriously empty even
though it was almost peak season, and
the farther she got, the more her spirits
rose. Freedom was a heady feeling and
she'd forgotten what it was like. She'd

nobody to please but herself, no plan in her head except to look up Jack Coverack. She owed that to Dan Warner who'd been as good as his word. Archdales had added one thousand pounds to her savings and been satisfied with just two weeks' notice. Besides, this Jack Coverack lived in such a pretty-sounding place — Rosemullion Bay. It had a welcoming sound. Jack Coverack sounded a bristly character. She imagined him dark, bearded, brooding, a mystery man!

Approaching Cornwall's gateway, the splendid Tamar Bridge, she headed for the South coast, keeping an eye out for signs to Rosemullion. Breasting a hill, a sweeping view of the sparkling bay took her breath away.

'Magic, magic,' she breathed, as out of the corner of her eye she saw a signpost to Rosemullion flash by on her left. 'Oops, missed it.'

There was now a snaking line of traffic behind her so she took the next left turn, instantly regretting it. There was hardly room for one car, let alone two. Amy just prayed she wouldn't meet another vehicle. The lane seemed endless but it was probably no more than a mile before it ended, widening into a small field where several cars were parked on the grass. She parked her car, too. A bed-and-breakfast board pointed left down a rutted track. She took the right hand coastal path. Maybe she'd have a cream tea later. Her early start meant there was plenty of time to explore before deciding where to stay.

The cliff path led uphill through a field, over a stile, into a small wood, then, dropped her on the edge of a headland looking down on a harbour, busy with boats and yachts of all shapes and sizes. A jumble of houses and cottages backed the water and a stone quay jutted out beyond the village. That surely must be Rosemullion. There would be lots of accommodation down there. It looked idyllic.

Turning her gaze away from the

harbour, the summer sea shimmered on her left, while sheep-dotted green fields on her right led gently upwards to a red and white striped beacon. Just below the beacon, off the path, a figure stood near an easel, scanning the horizon through a pair of binoculars. As Amy approached, the man turned as though expecting someone and raised his hand in greeting.

'Good morning,' Amy called out. 'Could you tell me, please, is that Rosemullion down there?'

He dropped the glasses and looked at her.

'It is. Are you lost?'

'Not really. I took a wrong turning farther back, so I wasn't sure.'

The man put the binoculars in a rucksack.

'The way to the village is back the way you came, through the wood and you'll see some steps. They lead to the beach at the edge of the village.'

He was scrutinising her curiously.

'I'll show you if you like. I'm going

back there myself.'

'Er, I'm not sure. I haven't decided yet.'

To avoid his gaze she moved towards the easel.

'You a painter?' she asked unnecessarily.

He laughed ruefully.

'Can't you tell? I'm not, but I've always wanted to try. I'm on a painting holiday and this is today's assignment. What do you think?'

'Er . . . very nice. Is it Rosemullion?'

'You don't have to be polite. I know it's pretty dreadful.'

'If you enjoy it . . . '

Amy wondered why he'd been scanning the horizon when the sketch was actually an unsuccessful attempt to depict the picturesque jumble of roofs and whitewashed cottages in inland Rosemullion.

'Very diplomatic.'

He put out his hand.

'Ben Peterson.'

His grip was warm, his smile friendly,

sunglasses on top of thick blond hair, very deep blue eyes in a tanned face. She reckoned he was in his early thirties or late twenties.

'You here on holiday?' he asked.

'Sort of,' she replied. 'Have you been here long?'

'A week or so. It's pretty full in Rosemullion, and there's a heatwave forecast so there'll be hordes of tourists expected at the weekend.'

'Maybe I'll look for somewhere off the beaten track, a bit quieter.'

'You won't find anywhere prettier to stay.'

'I don't need to stay in Rosemullion. I just need to see someone there.'

'Who would that be?'

'You can't know him, not if you're a tourist.'

'You'd be surprised. It's a small place, friendly, and I'm staying bang in the centre with a local family. Try me.'

Amy frowned. There was a quiet persistence about him, and something else that she couldn't figure.

'Jack Coverack,' she said hesitantly. 'He has a studio and a craft workshop.'

Ben Peterson froze, his gaze intensified, his eyes fractionally narrowed, then he pulled down his sunglasses, bringing down a barrier.

'Well, there's a coincidence. I do know Jack. Matter of fact, he's the one responsible for that gaudy daub.'

He lifted the painting from the easel and bent to put it away.

'He's my art teacher. I can take you to him any time you like.'

3

Amy stared in disbelief. She'd pictured Jack Coverack as a bit of a maverick. Art teacher pricked the illusion.

'I thought he was some sort of entrepreneur . . . business ventures.'

'Did you? And who gave you that idea?'

'That's how he was described, but it doesn't matter. It's not important. Perhaps you'd give me his address.'

'Better still, I'll show you. Come on.'

He hoisted his rucksack over his shoulder and tucked the folded easel under his arm. Amy hesitated. She hadn't reckoned on a guide and she knew nothing about this man. Since the Greenfingers' debacle her confidence had been shaken. Still, Ben Peterson looked harmless and he was only offering to show her Jack Coverack's place.

'My car's back at the cliff-top carpark.'

'Good, you can give me a lift down to Rosemullion. It's not far but I've had enough exercise for one day.'

It was a comment which Amy thought belied his lean, athletic body. Here was a man used to physical activity. He adapted his long stride to hers as they set off down the hill.

'Shall you be staying in Rosemullion?' he enquired casually.

'I don't know. I haven't made any plans.'

'There's a vacancy at Gull Cottage where I'm staying. Young couple moved on this morning.'

'I'm not sure. I ought to see Jack Coverack.'

'Is it urgent?'

'No, but it's the reason I dropped by Rosemullion.'

'Rosemullion isn't the sort of place you drop by. You stay and savour it, and you'll fall in love with Gull Cottage. Everyone does.'

'You sound like a local selling the place. Where's your home?'

'I move around.'

She sensed that Ben Peterson was keener on asking questions than answering them. She drove back towards the village. The road was narrow and high-hedged with a good deal of traffic and a steep descent to the harbour which required all her concentration.

'Left, left here.'

Ben's instruction was late. She swung wide to catch the turning. An oncoming car braked sharply but the tinkle of shattered glass told Amy her headlight had gone at least.

She leaned out of her window to speak to the other driver.

'I'm sorry. I was too far over.'

'My fault entirely,' Ben interrupted swiftly. 'I was too late in asking you to turn left.'

He got out.

'No damage to your car,' he said to the other driver.

'Shouldn't be. These cars are built like tanks.'

He climbed out to join Ben.

'No, not a scratch. Yours is a bit of a mess though.'

'It's not mine.'

Ben bent to examine the damage.

'Not too bad. Need a new headlight though.'

'Do you want the details of my insurance?'

Amy joined the two men.

'What for? No damage done and I've had two charming apologies. Where I live I would've had a black eye for being in your way. It's been a pleasure to bump into you. No road rage down here, eh?'

He jumped back in his car, and Amy reversed gingerly away from his bumper and tucked her car well into the roadside.

'Thanks again.'

The other driver grinned and waved. 'Phew.'

Amy leaned back.

'That does it! A guy thanks us for bumping into him! What's this place got?'

'Magic,' Ben said simply, 'and now you'll have to stay and find out for yourself. You can't drive without lights. Carry on a couple of hundred yards and Gull Cottage is at the top of the hill. There's parking space and we can assess the damage. I'm sorry, Amy, it really was my fault.'

'No, I should have carried on and turned round later. A rotten bit of driving.'

They looked at each other and simultaneously burst out laughing.

'Something in the air. I told you, magic! And look, there's Morwenna in the garden.'

A dark-haired woman with her arms full of roses came down the front path from the cottage.

'Ben! I guessed you'd be back. I've baked scones, the kettle's on, and who's this you've found?'

Her smile was warm, her voice frankly curious.

'Amy Barton. She found me on the cliffs. I thought you had a vacancy but I see from your sign that you haven't.'

'Bless you, that's Mike. Forgot to change it. I've a lovely double overlooking the harbour. Would you like to see it, Amy, or tea first?'

'I wasn't planning to stay but we've just had a bump. I need the car lights fixed.'

'Andy Dunne, garage in the square. I'll ring right now.'

'I don't want to be a nuisance.'

Amy felt that things were being decided for her, albeit in the nicest possible way.

'No bother, he's my cousin. Do it straight away.'

She glanced at Ben, registered an imperceptible shake of his head and changed tack.

'Or leastways first thing tomorrow.'

She passed the roses to Ben.

'Bring those through into the kitchen, will you? Mind the thorns. You follow Ben, Amy.'

The hall, dark after the bright sunshine, smelled of rosemary and thyme, and a wonderful waft of home-baking. Amy inhaled deeply.

'That takes me back to baking day at our farm with Mum and Aunt Janet. It makes me quite homesick.'

'Where's that, dear?'

Morwenna put a plate of scones and a pot of cream on a laden tray.

'Yorkshire, a farm in the Dales. Let me help.'

'Gracious, no, you're a guest. Take Amy through to the garden, Ben. The terrace has a wonderful sea view.'

'Amy's come to see Jack Coverack.'

Morwenna paused, jam pot from the cupboard held mid air.

'Jack? Gracious, whatever would you be wanting with our Jack?'

'It's just a name someone gave me. Is he peculiar or something?'

Morwenna laughed.

'Not peculiar exactly but I suppose he's a bit of a character. You'll see when you meet him. Now you just tuck into my special Cornish cream tea. After tea, I'll show you your room.'

An hour or so later Amy leaned her arm on the windowsill of her double with harbour view and let out a contented sigh. Fate had decreed she stay in Rosemullion so she'd enjoy it. Her room was comfortably cosy with all the modern bits bang up to date — whirlpool bath and needle shower! She'd report back to Sue this was just the sort of place for the clientèle of Tailormade in the future.

'I need to walk off that tea,' she informed a passing seagull, 'and maybe find out where the mysterious Jack Coverack hangs out.'

There was still plenty of heat left in the day as she slipped out of Gull Cottage and knew at once why it was so named. A flapping flurry of seagulls whirling up from the harbour filled the air with their raucous calls.

'Noisy beggars,' Ben said from the wooden bench by the front door. 'They'll probably wake you at dawn.'

'I can sleep through most things. I don't much like early starts.'

'Going for a walk? I'll come and show you Jack Coverack's place.'

It was difficult to refuse. Tea time had been fun and Ben had kept them entertained with travellers' tales. He seemed to have been everywhere and yet, after a couple of hours, Amy knew nothing about him, where he lived, what he did for a living, where his family was, or even whether he had his own family — a wife, perhaps children?

He hadn't given away a thing, cleverly steering talk around Morwenna and her fisherman husband, Mike, and drawing out Amy to talk about her childhood in the Yorkshire Dales. She glanced up at him. His face was relaxed, smiling as he pointed out local landmarks.

The town harbour was tranquil, bathed in the golden light of a summer's evening. Rosemullion sat on one side of an estuary opposite its sister village of Polmullion whose stone, sun-washed cottages across the deep-blue water mirrored those of Rosemullion. A couple of small ferries chugged between the villages, threading through the harbour traffic.

'It's beautiful,' Amy breathed, 'almost Mediterranean. I'm surprised you're not out painting it.'

'I expect Jack will get round to that one evening. Look, you can see his place from here. Follow the coast line to the right, a line of stone buildings out of the village. We'll walk up there.'

They followed the shoreline about half a mile beyond the harbour to a cluster of stone buildings. The nearest one had a slipway into the water.

'That's Coverack's place, a craftwork shop, studio, pottery, gift shop.'

'It's pretty ramshackle.'

Amy was doubtful. If this was Jack Coverack's entrepreneurial base it didn't impress her!

'Part of its charm. You wouldn't want plate glass and plastic here.'

'I suppose not. It looks deserted, too.

Odd there are no visitors.'

'Closed from four to eight every day. Jack doesn't believe in overwork, and Michela sort of runs the gift shop, when she isn't potting.'

'Michela?'

'His partner.'

'No point in coming if you knew he wasn't going to be here, was there,' Amy said rather cuttingly.

'I said the gift shop's closed. Jack might be around though. Let's see.'

The outside of the shop was attractive with bottle-glass windows and freshly-pointed stonework, but the closed sign was across the window and the lights off.

'There's a flat above. I'll ring the bell.'

He rang several times but there was no answer.

'Sorry, no luck, but he has to be here in the morning. The class starts at ten. We'll come back. Don't look so disappointed. What's the urgency?'

'I just want to get on with things.'

'What things?'

'Oh, business,' she said evasively. 'We should get back.'

'Why? There's a pub round the next bend, right on the water. I'll buy you a drink. Might even see Jack in there. It's his local.'

'For goodness' sake! Meeting him isn't important. Why do you keep pushing it? It's none of your business anyway. I hardly know you and you've done nothing but ask questions since I met you.'

Ben stepped back and threw up his hands in mock defence.

'Hey, sorry. I was just trying to help.'

'I don't need your help. I'm quite capable of seeing Jack Coverack on my own so don't think of nannying me in the morning. Perhaps I'd better carry on my walk alone as I originally intended.'

He dropped his hands, the smile left his face and he looked at her in a curiously speculative way.

'Fair enough, if that's what you want. I'll leave you.'

She nearly called him back, ashamed of her outburst. Curiosity was natural and she was curious about him, piqued he kept up his guard while trying to lower hers. She'd been childish.

'Ben,' she called after him but either he didn't hear or chose not to.

She carried on walking, wishing Ben hadn't gone. However, the pub looked inviting. Lots of people, families, couples, groups of friends enhanced her loneliness. Usually she liked her own company but now the prospect of sitting alone clutching a glass of wine was unappealing. She'd ring Sue from the pub and then go back to Gull Cottage and make it up with Ben. But when she returned to the cottage, he had gone.

'Gone fishing with Mike,' Morwenna told her, 'and knowing those two it'll be the small hours before they're back.'

'Has he been here long?' Amy probed. 'He acts like a local.'

'A week this time but he's backwards and forwards. Will you be wanting any supper?'

'Where's he from?'

'You know, I'm not so sure. I've fresh-baked pasties. No more than a minute or two to heat up.'

If Morwenna knew anything about Ben, she wasn't telling. A discreet landlady or had she had instructions? Amy yawned.

'Sorry. A pasty sounds wonderful but I'm still full of that lovely tea. This air's making me sleepy so I think I'll have an early night. What time's breakfast?'

'Just whenever you're ready, my dear. Sleep in all you want to.'

'I'll be up early to see Jack Coverack.'

'That'll make your day for sure.'

Morwenna's tone was deliberately bland. She couldn't help wondering what someone like Amy Barton wanted with Jack.

Amy woke and for a second couldn't think where she was. Blazing sunlight flooded into the room but it was the discordant shriek of gulls which brought memory streaming back. She groped for her watch and shot upright.

Nine thirty! Half the morning gone. She leaped out of bed. She had to see Jack Coverack! Once that was out of the way she could move forward, formulate a plan.

Savoury smells of coffee and bacon greeted her but no sign of a soul at Gull Cottage. A note propped on the kitchen table told her that breakfast was in the Aga. Morwenna had had to go to market so Amy had to help herself. Amy's eyes popped when she saw the size of breakfast but she managed to make creditable inroads into the creamy, scrambled eggs, bacon, sausage and home-baked bread.

Well fortified, she set out to get the Jack Coverack meeting out of her system. There was no sign of Ben Peterson. There were lots of holiday-makers out and about and most of them seemed to have ended up at Jack Coverack's premises. The gift shop was crowded but as far as Amy could see there were no assistants to serve or help them. For some reason she felt nervous.

The mysterious Coverack had had such a build up she half expected some bogey man of childhood nightmares to leap out at her. She almost wished Ben was there to ease the introduction.

The visitors seemed relaxed and content to browse around the oddly-assorted jumble of souvenir tack and up-market gifts. Galleons in bottles, plaster gnomes and Cornish pixies jostled for space among the thick stone gift mugs. Some lovely delicate, hand-thrown pots lurked in corners on high shelves, and quality paintings hung side by side with garish oils depicting what Amy assumed were Rosemullion Harbour views. It was a real jumble of a gift shop and Amy's opinion of Jack Coverack's business sense plummeted. Patience was running out among the customers.

'Shop,' someone called loudly and banged a bell on the counter.

After a couple of minutes, a young woman appeared behind the counter, shaking clouds of a fine, powdery substance from her hair.

'So sorry, the kiln — I had to finish.'

Her manner was vaguely distracted but she polished off the shopful of customers efficiently enough until Amy was the only one left.

'Yes? I'm sorry you had to wait.'

'I'm not buying right now,' Amy said. 'I'm here to see Jack Coverack.'

'Jack? He's teaching, in the studio. He'll be another hour probably. Would you like to wait? I'm not sure what he's doing. I could go and see.'

'God give me strength!'

An angry voice interrupted, accompanying clattering footsteps on uncarpeted wooden stairs. A door burst open and a scowling man just about got his broad frame through the low, narrow doorway.

'That's it! I've had it with those would-be painters up there. Not a grain of talent amongst them. What's the point? Coffee, Michela, and I might just be able to go back.'

'Hush.' The woman put her fingers to

50

her lips. 'They'll hear you. They've paid good money for their tuition, and there's someone here to see you.'

Amy had moved away, pretending to be absorbed in a particularly gaudy seascape. She turned round and she saw with a jolt that the man, presumably Jack Coverack, was indeed what she'd imagined — dark, Celtic, piratical-looking and smouldering with annoyance.

'And who might you be?' he almost barked.

'Amy Barton. Dan Warren gave me your name.'

'Dan? Why didn't you say?'

'I didn't get a chance. If you're busy I'll go. It's not important.'

'No, don't. I owe Dan Warren. What is it you want?'

The glower was still there but marginally softer since the mention of Dan.

'He just thought you might just have a few ideas about business . . . a job.'

It sounded absurd and Amy wished

she'd never come. How on earth could this man help her?

'But I see it was foolish. I won't waste your time.'

'Hold on,' he commanded. 'What sort of business?'

'Oh, anything. Gift shop, plants . . . '

'There are too many gift shops. This county's saturated with them. Dan must be out of his head.'

The doorbell went and several customers piled in. For a few minutes Michela was busy and Jack Coverack was drawn into discussion on one of the better paintings on the wall. Amy made a move to go but Jack caught her arm as she made for the door.

'Wait,' he said brusquely.

Jack Coverack's manner was commanding rather than encouraging and she felt her hackles rise. When the shop was empty again the dark man looked consideringly at her.

'What did you do before, and what's your connection with Dan?'

'Partner in a garden centre. I was

made redundant in a take-over. It was Dan Warren who had to break the news to me. I guess he felt sorry for me and he recommended you.'

She matched his brusqueness.

'You're not expecting to open a garden centre here, I hope. There are too many already, most of them just gift shops masquerading.'

'No, I'm not. I'm on holiday and looking around for ideas. I can't think what Dan was doing sending me here. A complete waste of time, and shouldn't you be getting back to your class? I was an art student once. I couldn't stand it when the tutor swanned off for hours.'

'A mere ten minutes, and it's coffee break. You've got an art diploma?'

'Yes. What's that got to do with anything?'

'If you're looking for work why don't you take this class yourself? I've had more than enough.'

'Jack, you can't . . . '

'Can't what, Michela?'

'You can't just ask a passing stranger to take over your class.'

'I just have. It's a golden opportunity. If you're looking for a business, a seaside painting school's a fine idea, if you can stand the students. I can't.'

'Why start the courses then?'

'Challenge at first but I soon got bored, and I've other things to do which are much more important. Will you do it?'

His deep eyes challenged her and a half smile on his lips softened the dour look.

'Only a couple more weeks. I'm going to cancel the next lot.'

Two weeks, why not? Mornings only, Ben had said. Not too arduous, with lots of time left for exploring, and one of Tailormade's plans was for creative holidays. She could do some research, test the market from the inside.

'Well? Come on, I'll introduce you to the class.'

'Now?'

'Why not? There's an hour or two

left. Get to know them. I'll give you a course outline and you'll just have to supervise.'

'OK, what's to lose?'

'Up we go then. My lucky day. Thanks, Dan.'

He practically propelled her up the steps.

'You are heavensent, Amy Barton.'

4

The soft knock made Amy jump and nearly drop the painting, which was excellent. Elaine Brady had talent but no confidence. Amy planned to foster the one and boost the other in the next class.

'Michela, come in. Tell me what you think of this.'

Obediently, Michela studied the seascape.

'Very good. Wonderful cloud effect. Your star pupil?'

'I think so. Mind you, and I have to say it, the standard's not great, but what the heck, they all enjoy it, except one.'

'That'll be Ben Peterson,' Michela said and laughed. 'Forget your class now. It's Friday night and you've worked hard. You need a break. There's wine, home-made pâté and trimmings laid out on the patio. Tempted?'

'I should say so. That's really good of you. I'll tidy up in here.'

'Don't be too long or the sun'll have moved off the patio.'

Amy shuffled Elaine's work into its folder. It had been a good week. She stretched out tense muscles. Although it was just over a week since she'd come to Rosemullion it felt as if she'd been there for ever. Greenfingers and Archdale seemed distant memories.

She'd seen little of Jack Coverack since he'd unceremoniously bundled her into his studio, introduced her as the new teacher and left. The first few hours had been tricky and there had been mutterings about refunds and unprofessional behaviour. It had been Ben Peterson who'd overridden the annoyance and suggested Amy be given a chance.

In spite of being just about the worst painter in the group he appeared to exercise some leadership and the class settled down to assess Amy's capabilities. It was a challenge she rose to easily, winning over the most awkward members after her first morning in the studio. Now, she felt very much part of the whole set-up, even giving Michela a hand in the gift shop or pottery. She locked the studio and ran downstairs.

Glasses and chilled wine were on the wooden table facing the sea and Michela was unloading a tray of food.

'Hi. We've two hours before the hordes of souvenir hunters descend. Friday night's always the busiest with people buying last-minute gifts. Here, help yourself. You've earned it.'

Michela sliced a crusty brown cob, speared a thick slice and put it on Amy's plate.

'You've got to try this, from the local bakery, walnut and rosemary. I love it, Jack hates it.'

Amy bit into the thickly-buttered bread.

'I don't know him at all,' she said cautiously, wondering for the umpteenth time what the relationship was between Michela and Jack.

The brief time she'd seen them together she'd noted an interdependence though Jack always seemed the dominant one. Michela's easy friendliness had made Amy feel very much at home in the village from the outset, yet in spite of that, she felt a reserve which precluded personal questions.

'Great bread. The sort you could eat and eat. Fatal!'

'It is, and I do. So, how's your week been? There's good feedback from the students who come into the shop. They like you.'

'That's good. Bit of a gamble though. Is Jack given to impulses? I mean, to abandon his class to a complete stranger is a bit odd to say the least.'

Michela hesitated, busying herself in slicing more bread. She avoided Amy's eyes and her words came reluctantly.

'Jack is an unusual man. He does act on impulse, and he has hunches about people. He must trust you because he'd never let his class down unless he was sure.'

'But he knows nothing about me.'

'He can tell,' Michela persisted but Amy thought it unlikely.

'But he doesn't paint and he's never here to see to the business.'

'Just at present he has a few problems,' she said then tailed off.

'I'm sorry. It's none of my business. I'm too nosey, and he seems to do OK. That yacht in the harbour, Ben pointed it out, it's really flashy.'

'That's not his personally, it's business. Ah, here's Ben.'

Michela's relief was obvious as Ben's shadow fell across the table.

'Sit down, Ben, and I'll get more wine and bread.'

'Thanks, it looks too good to pass up, but I really came to apologise to ma'am here. I'm sorry I couldn't make the class today, Amy.'

'What's your excuse this time? Fishing again? You'll never make any progress if you miss half the classes. It's your choice, you're paying, but I don't think you're terribly interested in painting.'

Ben looked sheepish and slid a couple of tasty prawns into his mouth.

'That's not very encouraging, Miss Barton.'

'I can't encourage what's not there,' Amy said severely.

'That's reasonable. I'll do better next week. Honest! You are staying on?'

'I don't have an option. It wouldn't be fair to go, unless Jack returns.'

She looked at Michela.

'No. I know he doesn't want to take the class, and you are enjoying it, Amy, aren't you?'

'Yes, yes, I am, but I should think of moving on.'

'What for?' Ben asked.

'Things to sort out,' she said lamely, disconcerted by the intensity of his blue eyes as he stared at her.

'But as you're still here and it's the weekend why don't we go out tomorrow? A picnic by the sea? The forecast's hot and sunny.'

It was tempting. She turned to Michela.

'You'll come, too?' she said.

'Couldn't possibly, I've got to see . . .'

Michela stopped abruptly. She felt so easy and comfortable with Amy the words had nearly slipped out but Jack had warned, not a word to anyone, the situation's bad so don't make it worse by spreading it about.

'. . . to see the shop,' she improvised, 'and I plan to fire the kiln tomorrow. You two go enjoy yourselves. It's going to be a beautiful weekend. Ben, open this other bottle, please. I think it's just about cold enough.'

On Saturday morning Amy and Ben set off from Gull Cottage in Ben's open-topped car, the only kind of vehicle, he said, for such an outing.

'Where are we going?'

She slung a rucksack on the back seat and tied back her hair.

'Surprise. Mystery tour,' Ben replied as he slipped on dark sunglasses.

'As I don't know anywhere outside Rosemullion anywhere's a mystery.'

'So, relax and enjoy the day.'

He laid his arm across the back of her seat as he reversed out of the Gull Cottage parking space. Amy felt his fingers brush her neck.

They were soon out of the village, climbing the coast road, the sea glittering its best deep turquoise. There was not a speck of cloud and a soft breeze caressed Amy's cheeks. She smiled.

He pointed to the yachts out to sea.

'Regatta week. Races today. Do you sail?'

'No. There was always so much to do on the farm. Do you?'

'I've a boat moored up river from Rosemullion.'

'Here? But I thought you went fishing in Mike's boat.'

'Sometimes his, sometimes mine. If the weather holds I'll take you out in Lucinda if you like.'

'I would, but you don't live around here, do you?'

'No reason for not bringing my boat down.'

'Where from?'

'Oh, up country,' he said vaguely. 'Look, up on the cliff you can just glimpse chimney pots. That's Chalfrey Manor, where we're going.'

'A manor? I thought we were going swimming.'

'That, too. You'll see.'

He swooped the open car up and down narrow, twisting lanes, sometimes the high Cornish hedges completely hiding the view, then miraculously the road ran clear to skirt low cliffs and golden sand.

'Off the main tourist route, and here it is.'

He slowed before a pair of high iron gates flung open.

'Chalfrey Manor, gardens open to the public on certain days, for charity. This happens to be one of those days.'

Ben crunched the car up a long, gravel drive flanked by masses of rhododendrons and camellia bushes.

'Spectacular in the springtime. There's the house. That's not open to the public

64

but maybe I can arrange a quick tour if you're into that sort of thing.'

'Wow, it's a castle!' Amy exclaimed. 'Those crenellated towers are marvellous. I'd love to go in. Do you know the owners?'

'No. We'll do the gardens first.'

Amy had seen around lots of gardens as consultant at Greenfingers but Chalfrey's gardens were something else. The mixture of formal Victorian and romantic wildness was enchanting, the rose garden perfection.

'It's lovely. You're clever to find this place away from the tourist beat.'

'Tomorrow will be busier, ice cream and roundabouts.'

'Is there a family living here now?'

'Yes. Descendants of the original.'

'Lucky them. This garden's a dream.'

'There's a herb garden through there. You feast your eyes and nose on that and I'll see if I can fix a look at the house.'

'You've been here before?' she asked immediately.

'Um, no.'

The hesitation was so fractional Amy wondered if she'd imagined it.

'It's in the guide book,' Ben added, too glibly. 'Shan't be long.'

The herbs' perfume was dizzyingly erotic, the fragrances of sage, marjoram and lavender wafting on the warm air and she inhaled the scents deeply as she wandered through massed banks of fennel and borage. She sat on a warm, stone seat, closed her eyes and lifted her face to the sun.

Something about Ben was troubling her. He wasn't telling the truth. He was too familiar with Chalfrey Manor's layout not to have been here before, and how could he arrange a personal tour if he didn't know anyone there? Secrets? Chalfrey must be choked with past secrets, peopled with ghosts. As she relaxed, she could feel the ghosts floating round her in the soft summer air. She felt she could touch them. Putting up a hand she gasped as it was taken and held.

'Amy! What's wrong? You're miles away. I've fixed up a whirlwind tour.'

Ben hauled her upright and tucked her arm in his.

'Half an hour and then we'll swim. We can use Chalfrey's private beach.'

★ ★ ★

Amy exhaled a deep sigh of contentment and wriggled her toes deeper into the hot sand. Behind closed lids she recalled images of Chalfrey Manor. Ben had literally whizzed her through the beautifully-furnished rooms, a long gallery and a book-lined library with a sweeping view of blue bay and green cliffs. She'd lingered among the books and portraits.

'There isn't time now,' Ben said, sweeping her along impatiently. 'We'll come back another time.'

'Why did we bother then? I can't take all this in in thirty minutes. There're centuries of stuff to absorb. It's crammed with antiques. Is anyone about?'

'A couple of caretakers. I spoke to them earlier. Come on, Amy, it's far too hot to be indoors and that sea's screaming for attention.'

Grumbling faintly, Amy had allowed herself to be dragged away from the delights of the manor and followed Ben out into the sunlight. He was 'way ahead, his long legs easily outpacing her. She broke into a run. Ben turned, waving her towards a small copse. He was unlocking a wooden gate when she caught up with him.

'Now,' he said, 'you can see why I was impatient to be here.'

She took a few steps forward.

'Careful,' Ben said and held her back. 'These first steps are steep.'

She looked cautiously over the edge of the cliff. Rough steps led down on to rocks guarding a perfect cove. Rock pools lower down fringed a semicircle of almost white sand lapped by deep blue ripples.

'Magic,' she whispered, aware of Ben close behind her, his hands on her shoulders.

'I keep telling you — magic land.'

His voice was low, almost caressing.

'Race you into the water,' he called, scrambling down the cliff at speed.

Amy followed more slowly with no intention of competing. She watched him on the beach carelessly stripping off jeans and T-shirt, leaving them in an untidy heap before taking a racing plunge into the sea. She registered his tanned, muscular figure before he hit the waves, then slipped off her shorts and shirt and walked into the water to join him. They swam around in the clear, cool water for about twenty minutes then decided to eat.

Morwenna had packed a mammoth picnic of pasties, salad, cheese and fruit and Ben had plunged a bottle of wine in a cool, deep-shaded pool earlier. He now drew the wine cork with a satisfying plop.

Amy looked out to the blue horizon.

'Ben, how did you get the key to the gate at the top of the steps?'

'Influence. It goes with the tour.'

'You said you'd never been here before.'

'Did I?'

His gaze followed hers into the distance. He turned and touched her lips.

'You ask too many questions. Enjoy the moment.'

'I am, but I'd like to know about you, too. You're giving me a perfect day but I know nothing about you, who you are, what you're doing here.'

'Isn't it now that matters? Why is it so important?'

He knew it was unconvincing but there was no way he could or would answer Amy's questions. Usually he was adept at evasion, but this time it was difficult. He saw her puzzled frown as she bit her lip.

'Natural curiosity, if you like someone.'

He compromised a fraction.

'I've a base in London, I travel a lot, I'm on a painting holiday. You may snort but it's true. Why else would I be taking classes?'

'I'm not sure.'

He leaned across and gently pulled her back on to the sand and took her hand in his, exerting soft pressure on her fingers.

'It might rain tomorrow,' he said, 'then you'll regret wasting this afternoon on interrogation.'

Amy burrowed into the sand's heat, aware of Ben's hand in hers, also aware of the tension between them. He withheld too much of himself. He was charming and he attracted her but the central core was a mystery, and one he wasn't prepared to divulge. It was impossible for her to relax completely with so many questions buzzing in her head but she lay quietly for a while, very conscious of Ben's closeness. She directed her mind to drift, to let go of the mystery, then suddenly she sat bolt upright.

'Then there's Jack Coverack,' she exclaimed suddenly.

She felt Ben's hand tighten over hers.

'What do you mean?'

His voice sounded wary.

'It's a strange set-up. He's never there, and Michela — are they partners in life, not just business. There's something personal between them.'

Ben sat up, released her hand.

'How should I know? Their relationship's none of our business.'

'I do work for him.'

She felt his hostility like a sting.

'Ask him yourself if you're so interested.'

He stood up.

'I've had enough third degree for one day. I'm going back in the water. I've left the masks and snorkels in the car. I'll fetch them. No, you stay here, finish the wine.'

Before Amy could argue, he was gone, picking up jeans and shirt as he went. If he stayed much longer, the girl's questioning would get to him.

72

Besides he had to go back to the house. On the rocks he turned and waved. Amy waved back, relieved. For a few seconds she'd thought he'd had the look of a man who didn't intend to return! Silly notion. He wasn't the sort of man to abandon her on a remote beach. She lay down to sunbathe.

An hour later, Ben still hadn't returned. The car couldn't be more than fifteen minutes away, twenty at the outside. She saw the tide had turned and was advancing rapidly towards their picnic spot. The sun was more hazy, the sky no longer bright blue. A cool breeze made her shiver.

Pulling on shirt and shorts she picked up the picnic things, stuffed towels and rugs into rucksacks and left them at the bottom of the steps. It wouldn't take a minute to retrieve them later. She felt the chill of her slightly damp swimsuit. She'd be glad of her sweater in the car.

The car was there, locked, with its top now on, sweater and snorkels on the back seat, and there was no sign of

Ben. A few people strolled the gardens but Ben wasn't among them. She tried the house. The front was deserted, the massive entrance door shut. Round the back there were clusters of outbuildings and a door ajar led into a stone-slabbed dairy which led into an unexpectedly high-tech kitchen.

'Hello. Anyone there?'

Her tentative call echoed eerily and went unanswered. Just as she was about to go back and wait for Ben by the car she thought she heard movements overhead, distant voices. The kitchen gave way to a long corridor with wide stairs at the end. The voices were nearer now and with relief she recognised one of them as Ben's. She ran up the stairs to a swing door and was about to push it open when she heard her own name.

'Amy, the girl I came with, will still be on the beach. I made an excuse but she'll be expecting me back. You were late.'

The other voice, male, was quieter. She couldn't catch the words. The tone was questioning, followed by Ben's easy laugh.

'Of course she doesn't suspect. Why should she? Mind you I'd give a lot to know what she's up to, and what's her connection to Coverack.'

Amy's hand flew to her mouth. She stepped back, instinct warning her not to be caught snooping. She turned to go but the voices had stopped right the other side of the door. Then the other voice came, clearer now.

'It's the ideal spot, Uncle Fred's folly. Fred was a colourful eccentric who thought the cold war would end in Armageddon so he built his very own nuclear bunker here in one of the cellars, and it's impossible to find unless you know just where to look.'

Amy willed them to move on so she could escape back to the car but they seemed rooted to the danger spot outside her door. She prayed the cellars weren't through the kitchen, then wondered why on earth Ben was interested in Uncle Fred's bunker. She held her breath. Every word carried through the door.

'You're quite sure about this?' Ben said. 'If things get out of hand it could be dangerous. You don't have to do it.'

'Ben, I owe you more than one favour, and don't forget Alice and I are off to Tuscany for a month. We'll know nothing about it, and I'll deny every-thing if necessary. Go ahead, stash the stuff. Uncle Fred'd be tickled pink.'

'If you're really sure?'

'Certain. By the way, Lucinda's coming back. Had a great time. Our grandchildren certainly love adventures, and none more than Lucinda.'

The voices were moving on at last.

'I know, she's written. I'm meeting her at Heathrow.'

'Are you? I'm delighted. She's crack-ers about you, Ben. You must know.'

The closing of the door cut off the rest and Amy exhaled slowly, trying to make sense of what she'd heard. So, Ben was up to something, something dangerous, even illegal maybe? And who was Lucinda, who had the same name as his boat, and was crackers about him, and where was this nuclear bunker? She knew it would be no use asking Ben, but now she knew he had something to hide. She stood, irresolute, then impulsively pushed open the swing door. It wouldn't hurt just to follow the two men, see if they let drop any more information. Soft-footed, she went after them.

It was a silly mistake, she realised almost immediately. She should have turned and fled back to the garden as soon as Ben and his companion had gone. What an idiot to think she could possibly have found out anything by following them. There was no sign of them, and now she was lost.

The place was a maze of corridors, stairs and dead ends, bearing no resemblance to the place she'd visited that morning. She had to get out but couldn't find any exits. It was all a nightmare of long corridors and stained-glass windows giving no clue to whether she was at the front or the back of the house, or what floor even.

Despairingly, and with little hope, she pushed open yet another heavy door, finding more steps, another door. She must be well below the basement level. Thank goodness — a blast of cool air and stone steps leading down to a room where shafts of light meant access to the outside world couldn't be far away. She stepped forward eagerly, missed the steps and fell, crying out in pain as her spine bounced down the concrete steps.

Darkness shut out the sunlight, the heavy door at the top of the steps swung shut, but she'd passed out, and didn't hear the self-locking system click into place.

5

Working out an excuse for the delay, Ben picked up the masks and snorkels from the car and ran through the wood to the cliff top. He'd forgotten how fast the tide raced in across the shallow sand. Water lapped the lower steps, and there was no sign of Amy!

He'd pointed out another cove half a mile back on the way in. Maybe she was there. He sprinted up the steps and broke into a powerful run along the cliff top but there was no sign of her. Where was she? If she'd gone back to the house surely he'd have seen her. He frowned.

As he returned to their picnic beach he glanced down, and froze. The tide had turned and floating out to sea were Amy's towel and rucksack. He dashed down the steps. The towel and bag bobbed away from him. There was no sign of Amy's swimsuit.

'Amy!' he called, with a note of desperation.

The rip tide could spring up with vicious speed. Had he warned her? He couldn't remember. In seconds he was in the sea, swimming beyond the headland. It was choppier, the wind gusting. He trod water, whirling round, searching, but there was no sign of her. He swam back to the shore. His mobile phone was in the car. He'd have to call the police, though the last thing he wanted was police attention on Chalfrey Manor, but concern for Amy had to take precedence.

Running to the car, he heard a sound more associated with city streets than quiet, Cornish lanes — police sirens! He drove at speed back to the house, coming to a screeching stop by the front entrance where small knots of people stood around, drawn by the police sirens.

'What happened?' he queried, leaving the car door swinging wide.

'Not sure,' a middle-aged woman replied, looking disapprovingly at his wet clothes and draggled hair. 'Seems there's been an accident. They brought out a girl, unconscious, I think, but I can't . . . '

She was speaking to the air. But Ben was already too late. The ambulance was speeding up the drive. He hesitated. A man was at the front door. Ben ran up the steps.

'No visitors allowed in the house.'

The man tried to close the door. Ben put his foot against it.

'No, wait, I'm not a visitor. I'm a friend of Sir Roy's. I was with him earlier. You're the caretaker?'

'Yes. My wife and I have been away. We came back to close up the house.'

'Sir Roy?'

'Gone. We only saw him for a few minutes. He's gone back to London. They're going to Tuscany. I'm glad he didn't find her. Gave me a shock, I can tell you. If we'd left, closed up, God knows how long she'd have lain there.

Quite by accident I went down there.'

'The girl, what did she look like?'

'No idea. She was out for the count.'

'Did she have wavy reddish hair and blue eyes?'

'Certainly reddish hair, good figure. Eyes were closed. Young, she was, and white as death.'

'OK. Thanks.'

Ben ran back to the car. Of course it was Amy, of course she'd have gone back to the house. It all tied in. She came from Bath, knew Jack Coverack. She'd played the innocent very well indeed. Anger clouded his worry for Amy's personal safety as he drove grimly in the direction the ambulance had taken.

When he arrived at the hospital and gave Amy's name, the girl at the desk clicked through her computer.

'Admitted a quarter of an hour ago?'

'Yes. Is she badly hurt?'

'I couldn't say. She's being assessed. You a relative?'

'No, I . . .'

'In that case, I'm not allowed to give information.'

'But I've been with her all day, and it's my fault she's hurt.'

Ben put on a persuasively anxious expression and she softened.

'Take a seat and I'll see what I can find out. May take a while.'

Ben was not good at waiting and he had too many questions he needed answers to. It seemed an age and it was several cups of dreadful coffee later that the receptionist pointed a young doctor in Ben's direction.

'Mr Peterson? You were asking about Amy Barton.'

'Yes. How is she?'

'Conscious, but seriously bruised. We're keeping her in overnight, usual precaution in case of concussion. You're not a relative?'

'No, no. I'd just like to see her, please. I followed the ambulance. We'd been out together for the day.'

'Well, just for a few minutes, as there's no family here apparently. If she's OK in the morning she'll be discharged, though someone should be with her for a couple of days.'

'I can arrange that.'

'We've contacted a cousin in Bath. Ms Barton didn't want her parents bothered. She was in shock when she came in, but she should be fine. She's in Ward 3. Make it brief.'

Ben walked soft-footed into the four-bed ward. Amy, in a bed by the window, lay perfectly still, eyes closed, her alarming pallor matching the hospital sheets. He took her hand. Her eyes opened, she smiled, and he took her in his arms, relief washing over him as he kissed her on the lips. He felt a small jolt of surprise.

'Why did you go back to the Manor? What were you doing in the cellar?'

Anxiety made his tone abrasive.

'You were away so long. What were you doing?'

'I thought you'd drowned. Your things were in the sea.'

He remembered his panic in the

water searching for her when all the time she'd been in the house, doing what? Looking for what?

'Why were you in that cellar?' he repeated.

'I couldn't find my way out and I got lost in the maze of corridors, then I felt an air current so I opened a door and fell down the steps. I didn't intend to. I was trapped, I suppose.'

'That door locks from the inside, but there's a key by the steps.'

'How do you know that?'

Amy struggled to sit up, and winced.

'What did you find out?' Ben, cursing his slip of the tongue, spoke harshly. 'And why did you follow me?'

'I've told you, I was cold and bored.'

'What did you see, in the Manor?'

He gripped her hand tightly. So, she had followed him.

'Anything? Anybody?'

'No, no. What should I have seen? Let go my hand, Ben, you're hurting. And what were you doing there?'

'So you did see me?'

'No. No, I didn't.'

A half lie — she'd heard him.

'What are you up to, Amy Barton?'

'I could ask you the same.'

Her colour had returned and for a moment she forgot her pain.

'You're no art student, and you're not at Rosemullion for a painting holiday,' she continued.

'You should leave Rosemullion,' Ben's voice whispered, 'and you should certainly leave Jack Coverack's employment.'

'Jack Coverack? Leave him? Whatever for? I'm committed to him for the next few weeks. Anyway, what's it to do with you?'

'He's bad news. You should keep away from him.'

'Why is he? You should mind your own business and . . . aah.'

Pain shot through her as she tried to move and a nurse came running.

'What's going on? If you two want to fight, kindly wait until the patient's fit. You,' she said to Ben, 'should be ashamed of yourself.'

She felt Amy's pulse and tut-tutted.

'Much too rapid. You need rest, not a slanging match. You, please go.'

'But I . . . ' Ben protested.

'Go, now, before I call Security.'

He looked furious but there was nothing he could do but obey.

'Sorry. I'll see you, Amy,' he said softly.

'Not if I can help it,' Amy muttered.

'That's was no way for adults to behave,' the nurse grumbled, 'though I admit your young man's very attractive. I expect he's just beside himself with worry about you. They often show it in anger. Now you must rest, and get ready for him taking you home tomorrow. I'll get your medication.'

'He's not . . . I don't . . . Oh, what's the use?'

Amy groaned. What a terrible mess, a wretched end to a perfect day! Heavily sedated, Amy slept for hours.

In the morning, the events since her

tumble were hazy. Vaguely she remembered Ben coming to the hospital, a quarrel, but she couldn't recall what it was about. There was something else, too. The kiss! Ben had kissed her and she'd kissed him back. What had that been about? Frowning, she tried to piece it all together as doctors and nurses came and went with batteries of tests. A doctor and Sue arrived together in the afternoon.

'Amy, what've you been up to?'

The cousins hugged each other.

'Don't ask. I'm so glad to see you. I hope you weren't worried.'

'I was to begin with, but I phoned last night quite late and you were dead to the world, not in any danger although you need looking after.'

'I'm sure I don't, but I'm delighted to have you in Rosemullion for a few days. I can go home now, can't I, Doctor?' Amy pleaded.

'Yes, so long as your cousin keeps an eye on you for a couple of days.'

'Perfect.'

Amy threw back the covers, put her feet on the floor.

'Ah, it still hurts!'

'It will do, so take it easy.'

'These painkillers should help,' the doctor said, and handed her a prescription.

As Sue drove Amy back to Rosemullion, they exchanged news and gossip, although Amy said nothing about Ben. She was still trying to reconcile her feelings towards him.

'You can share my room at Gull Cottage. It's a double, and you'll just love Morwenna and Mike. Rosemullion is lovely.'

'It sounds as if you've found your niche already.'

Sue concentrated on the road. It was a cloudy day but traffic was heavy.

'Not really, but it does have something special. Once we're fixed up with Morwenna I'll take you to see Michela and maybe Jack if he's back. I don't know what he'll have done about the students.'

'Goodness, you really are part of the place. What students, and shouldn't you be taking it easy? Tell me about it later.'

'I feel better already. Oh, up the hill, and here we are, Gull Cottage, Rosemullion. Isn't it wonderful?'

★ ★ ★

'Amy Barton, what a fright you gave us!'

Amy, engulfed in a great bear hug, was swung round and round the studio. She cried out in pain. Sue rushed forward.

'Put her down! She's hurt.'

Jack Coverack instantly released Amy, setting her down gently.

'Sorry, sorry. What an idiot. Will I never learn to think? But when Morwenna said you'd cracked your head on rocks on the beach . . . '

'No, no, it wasn't on the beach.'

How could Morwenna get it wrong?

'Never mind, you're back, and this is cousin Sue?'

Jack's most charming smile was put on for Sue's benefit.

'Glad to have you visit.'

He turned to Michela whose welcome to Amy was affectionate but much less boisterous!

'I shall take us all out to supper tonight, shut up shop and show Sue the best of the village.'

Sue was staring at Jack wide-eyed. She coughed.

'Er, shouldn't Amy rest?'

'Rest? She looks fine to me. Anyway, she can rest a while before we go out. Maybe I'll take Sue on a tour first.'

'No, no, I'll go back with Amy. We can meet up later.'

'As you wish. Six-thirty then, the Ship Inn.'

'What about the students?' Amy ventured.

'Oh, I sent them off on an assignment. You'll be able to assess what they bring back. See you all later then.'

A last flash of charm beamed directly at Sue, and he was gone.

'He's in a good mood. What's happened?' Amy wondered aloud.

Michela laughed.

'One of his schemes apparently coming together, he says. I don't know anything about it but we'll all have a good evening, that I guarantee. Now, how about some coffee?'

Michela was right, it was an extremely jolly evening. Jack was the perfect host, singling Sue out for high-octane charm, and wheedling Amy into almost agreeing to take the next painting class scheduled in two weeks' time. Amy wanted to explore other business possibilities in the South West but Jack dangled a tempting bait. He could fix a visit to a top chef in Devon for a few days before the painting course started. Cookery holidays, he maintained, would be ideal for a business interest, unwittingly putting his finger bang on the button of the cousins' dreams.

Back at Gull Cottage, the two girls discussed the evening.

'Jack's certainly taken with you, Sue. I've never seen him so relaxed and affable,' Amy said.

'What about Michela? Are they, well, partners?'

'Business only, I think, but this place is full of mysteries.'

'Such as?' Sue prompted as Amy appeared to have fallen into a trance.

'There's a guy, Ben Peterson,' Amy said reluctantly.

Ben had left Gull Cottage and Morwenna was evasive, saying she didn't know where he'd gone or for how long.

'He's very attractive, but I can't make up my mind. I don't think he is quite what he seems, in fact I know he's not.'

She stopped. Voices from below drifted through the open window.

'I don't like it,' Morwenna could be heard saying. 'Why tonight?'

Sue went to close the window, but, Amy stopped her, putting her fingers to her lips.

'I'll have to go, love. I'll need to bring

up the boat,' came Mike's voice.

'It's not fishing, is it?'

'Mebbe not,' Mike said, sounding cautious.

'Is he coming here?'

'No. After we've done what he wants us to do he's going straight back to London. Things are brewing.'

'I don't want to know,' Morwenna said. 'You shouldn't be involved.'

'I am already, and I'm not letting Ben down. We owe him, Morwenna.'

The voices went inside, dropping to a murmur.

'What was all that about?' Sue's expression spoke volumes. 'Is that the same Ben who's attractive, and why haven't you told me about him?'

'Because I wasn't sure what's going on. I still don't know, but one thing I do know is that Ben Peterson isn't just an ordinary guy in Rosemullion for a painting holiday. There's something decidedly fake about him. I bumped into him the first day I came to Rosemullion. He, and later, Jack, seemed to take charge of my life from then on. I was with Ben yesterday on a picnic but it all went wrong. Later, he came to the hospital, we had a row, and he was furious because I'd been inside Chalfrey Manor.'

'Chalfrey Manor?'

'I'll tell you about it later. I'm really worried, Sue. I think Ben's mixed up in something bad, maybe dangerous.'

'How? What sort of thing?'

Amy hesitated, hating to give the idea reality with words.

'I'm afraid . . . I think it could be drugs.'

'Drugs? Surely not. That's a bit melodramatic.'

'I know, but it's pretty common around here apparently. You know, lots of inlets, deserted creeks, so easy if you know the sea and rivers round here, and Ben's got a boat.'

Sue couldn't suppress a giggle.

'Don't look so tragic, Amy. Your problem is you watch too many movies. Half the population of Cornwall must own a boat of some sort and it doesn't make them drug smugglers.'

'Maybe I am being paranoid, but his behaviour at Chalfrey yesterday was so odd, and now he's gone away.'

'Hardly compelling evidence, cousin. You've not convinced me so far.'

'And he warned me off Jack,' Amy burst in. 'Said Jack was bad news or something like that.'

'Jack appears a good enough guy. A bit flamboyant but I liked him. Instinctively, I'd trust him.'

'Oh, yes, you and I, we're really good judges of character, aren't we? Remember Perfidious Tom, Two-Timing Gary? I'd say we were just about the last pair to pick out men of integrity.'

'Do you think whatever Ben's into involves Jack?' Sue asked.

'I've no idea. It obviously involves Morwenna and Mike, and I'd trust my life with those two.'

Sue looked rueful.

'That's a bad sign then. Tell me, what

exactly happened yesterday at Chalfrey Manor?'

The two girls talked well into the night without reaching any conclusions except that they should enjoy the next few days together, and that before the year was out they'd launch their travel business, Tailormade, and Amy was to take up Jack's offer of a week with the top Devon chef. Amy didn't admit it but she was relieved to think she'd be away from Rosemullion and its tantalising mysteries, for a while! She tried not to think too much of Ben.

6

Chef Bernard set down his final masterpiece of the cookery course, announcing, 'Braised shoulder of Devon lamb with scallop and sorrel stuffing. It's accompanied by wild blackberry and fennel sauce. You can now amaze your dinner party guests, even start your own restaurant. After all you've learned here, anything is possible.'

He stepped back and received a ripple of appreciative applause. Amy tried to forget how hungry she was and concentrated on her notes. The week had been a success. Jack's friend, Bernard, had been attentive and charming in spite of a packed schedule, and he'd demonstrated and taught a great respect for wonderful food along with a keen business sense of what would bump up the profits of his famous restaurant. Amy had confided her outline plans for Tailormade and he wanted to pin Amy down right away.

'Plans for next season, menus, trips, discounts . . . '

'Whoa, Bernard, we're nowhere near ready yet but I'm so impressed, you'll be top of our list as a venue for specialised holidays. It's just right for Tailormade. Specialised vacations at unique locations!'

'You should stay another week. I have a party from France so it will be spectacular.'

'I can't. I've loved it, but I have to get back.'

It wasn't true. The new intake of painting students wasn't due to start for five days. Bernard's French class might provide useful contacts, and European contacts would be important for Tailormade's future, but Amy couldn't quell a restlessness for Rosemullion. She was honest enough also to admit a need to see Ben so she could unravel the mystery in spite of a fear of what she might find.

That evening, she phoned Gull Cottage and next day arrived back in Rosemullion, to be greeted warmly by Morwenna.

'My goodness, you're looking better, Amy. No ill effects from that nasty tumble on the rocks?'

'Rocks? It wasn't . . . '

'You're in luck, my dear,' Morwenna interrupted eagerly, 'though I've had a rush of late bookings. It's the weather, I expect, just goes on and on. Drought warnings soon, I shouldn't wonder. Ben popped off yesterday, dunno where to so it's no good you asking, but I've moved his things into the cupboards and if he does come back we'll worry about that when it happens. Can't afford empty rooms. Good time in Devon?'

Morwenna paused for breath, and Amy took her opportunity.

'Do you expect him back soon?' she asked casually.

'Couldn't tell you. He never says.

Brought the boat up, went sailing. Had a young lady from London with him.'

'Lucinda?'

'Aye. Pretty name, pretty creature. Left here with some colour in her cheeks.'

'Lucinda? From Chalfrey Manor?' Amy persisted.

'London, I thought. Oh, and there's a message from Jack. Said to contact him as soon as possible.'

'I'll unpack, then go over right now.'

Amy was glad of something positive to do to erase the flat feeling of anticlimax. She hadn't realised how much she'd counted on Ben being at Rosemullion.

Jack greeted her exuberantly as though she was a long-lost friend. He'd prepared lists of students, timetables and topics to cover for the new course. Amy was amazed he was so well organised.

'Just a few suggestions. Ignore them if you like,' he said airily.

'Don't you want to take the course

yourself? You've put in a lot of work.'

'No, no, heaven forbid. Haven't the time nor the inclination, and there are more important events brewing. A guy from London's coming down tomorrow, business during the day and a little entertainment in the evening. I need your help. We'll shut up shop, take the boat out, have an evening swim and picnic. Michela, you as well.'

It was more of a command than an invitation, but Amy was pleased for the diversion. She was puzzled about Sue and Jack. When she'd telephoned her reports from Devon, Sue had dropped the news casually that Jack had been to Bath to visit. He'd taken her out to dinner and she'd enjoyed the evening. She'd been non-committal about the future and Amy hadn't pressed her. Nevertheless, her cousin was vulnerable and Jack Coverack so charming. Amy needed to find out more about him. Again Ben's warning flashed through her brain — he's bad news, keep away from him.

The evening began normally enough. It had been another perfect day though the barometer was dropping a bit. A mill-pond sea reflected the summer sun beginning to set. Michela had packed up food for a barbecue and Jack's yacht, moored in the harbour, was an expensive-looking craft. Jack handled it with practised ease.

'Once we're out in the bay we'll swim if you like. The water should still be warm. It's been a great summer.'

'How long before we get out there?' Jack's acquaintance asked.

Introduced merely as Ron from London, he looked ill-at-ease. Amy hadn't taken to him. He made no attempt to be friendly, indeed he seemed to resent the presence of the two women. Jack gave him a sharp look.

'Who says we're going anywhere special? Just a potter down the coast. Relax and enjoy the fresh air. It's a premium where you come from, Ron.'

'We do have other advantages.'

There was more than a sneer in Ron's voice.

'Can't think of a single one,' Jack replied with a dark frown.

'Not having the good fortune to live in the city how would you know?'

Amy spoke quickly to ease the tension.

'Wouldn't this be a good place to swim? There's a lovely sandy cove.'

She shaded her eyes. It was so familiar, the steps from the rocks, the cove, the little copse on the cliff. She looked up. The house would be out of sight from the sea.

'Isn't it Chalfrey Bay?'

Jack, busy dropping anchor, turned on her.

'Chalfrey Bay? You know it?'

'Of course. This is where I had the accident.'

'On the beach?'

'In the house. I foolishly got lost in there and fell down the cellar steps. Stupid of me.'

'You were inside the house?'

Jack's tone was incredulous and his dark eyes bored into hers.

'What were you doing there?'

Amy wished she'd never said anything. Ron looked at her very oddly.

'What's so strange? Ben took me on a picnic.'

She tried to speak lightly.

'You never mentioned that,' Jack snapped at Michela, who spread her hands in surprise.

'I didn't know. Is it important? All Morwenna told me was it was a fall on the rocks. Nothing about Ben or Chalfrey Manor.'

Jack's face was thunderous and for a few seconds looked about to erupt into fury. Then he blinked, shook his head and glared at Ron.

'No matter,' he said brusquely. 'If you want to swim, now's the time.'

The benign earlier mood, nearly shattered, reassembled as for the next half hour they all swam off the anchored yacht. Jack and Ron were the first to haul themselves back on board and when Amy and Michela joined them the two men were already dressed.

'We're going ashore,' Jack announced casually. 'I forgot the wine for supper. There's a place a mile or so along the coast. We'll take the dinghy. Could you start the barbecue? We shan't be long.'

'But I'm sure I packed the wine.' Michela frowned. 'In the cold box.'

But Jack was already over the side, the roar of the outboard motor drowning Michela's words. Amy watched them go.

'They're off to Chalfrey Beach. I don't remember a pub there,' she said.

'Jack knows the area well and he'll find a pub if there is one, but I could swear I packed the wine,' Michela replied.

'Don't worry about it. We'll start supper. That swim's given me an appetite.'

Amy was puzzled. Jack's reaction to her recognising Chalfrey was marked, and why had Ben concocted that story about the rocks? There were far more questions than answers, and how much did Michela know?

'Have you ever been to Chalfrey Manor?' she asked her as they prepared supper together in the smart, modern galley.

'Never heard of it before . . . whoops!'

The yacht rocked and plates and dishes slid across the surfaces.

'The sea's getting up a bit. Let's look.'

On deck, they saw the smooth sea was now ruffled with white flecks, its clear blue changed to black. The sun had dropped behind the horizon and the orange-streaked sky darkened.

'I hope Jack's not too long,' Michela said nervously. 'Do you know anything about boats? Are we supposed to put some lights on?'

'Not a thing, but I expect the lights are automatic. It's all pretty high-tech. I wouldn't like to touch any buttons.'

'There are quite a few boats around so that's reassuring.'

Michela pointed to the headland. 'Quite a cluster over there.'

'Probably had the same idea as us, evening swim and barbecue. Let's go back below and start cooking.'

The boat continued to rock, but more gently. The sausages began a slow sizzle, and Amy added chicken drumsticks.

'Hey.'

Michela's cry made her jump.

'I knew I'd put the wine in. It's under some boxes. I know I put it in the cold box.'

'Just be grateful it's there. Let's have a glass now.'

'OK, why not?'

Michela pulled the cork and poured deep red wine into two glasses.

'Leave the food on low. We'll take these into the lounge below.'

'Pretty de luxe,' Amy said as she stretched out on a deeply-upholstered bench which ran the length of a spacious lounge. 'Jack must do well out of whatever he does.'

'He seems to manage,' Michela answered.

'How long have you known him?'

Amy kept her tone light, seemingly politely interested.

'Not long, a couple of years.'

Amy decided to take the plunge.

'Tell me off for being nosy but are you two, well, I know you're business partners . . . '

'It's OK, Amy.' Michela laughed. 'You can't help being naturally curious. I don't mind, and no, no, we're not partners in any other sense. Didn't you see how taken he was by your cousin, Sue?'

'Well, I did, but I thought that maybe Jack's just a natural flirt. He's got an awful lot of charm when he's in the right mood.'

'True, but there's a dark side, too, although he's not a flirt. He likes Sue.'

She hesitated and took another sip of wine.

'I can trust you, can't I? Jack says it's best not to but . . . ' Michela paused.

'Sometimes I feel I'll die if I don't tell someone other than Jack.'

She broke off and buried her head in her hands. Amy reached forward.

'Hey, what's the matter?'

Michela's shoulders shook, tears flowed through her fingers, and she gasped for breath. Amy sat by her, putting her arm around her shoulders, alarmed at the unleashed emotion of the normally self-contained woman.

'Don't tell me anything if it upsets you,' Amy said.

'No, it's good for me, especially as it's nearly over. Give me a second.'

Amy waited in dread. What awful secret about Jack's business dealings would be revealed? Was Ben involved? Michela took a deep breath.

'What you see at the studio, shop, pottery, is a woman on her own absorbed in making pots in the beautiful surroundings of Rosemullion, contented and fulfilled.'

'That's what I see,' Amy agreed.

'It's only a part of reality. I have, or

did have, a husband and I have two children, a boy and a girl. Ranee is seven and Maya five. I haven't seen them for more than two years and it's killing me.'

'Michela! How?'

'My husband's Indian, and he's taken them to India, two years ago. Ours was a bad marriage. Everyone warned me but I was besotted. It didn't take long before the roses faded, but then there were the children. I tried, I failed, and we divorced. Ramon was bitter, but I thought he loved the children. He had access and one day he never brought them back. For two days I heard nothing, until the phone call from Delhi. He told me Ranee and Maya were Indian children now and absorbed into his family. I would never see them again. That was my punishment.'

'Punishment? For what?'

Michela shrugged.

'Being me, I suppose, daring to make a stand, wanting a career, whatever.'

'Didn't the police intervene?'

'The police made some attempts but the children were on Ramon's passport. The courts couldn't do a thing. I tried everything. I went to Delhi but there was no trace of the family.'

'And now?'

Michela smiled.

'Now, at last, I have some hope. That's why I can speak of it. And it's all because of Jack.'

'Jack?'

'A year ago, I came to Rosemullion in despair — no job, no money, no future. I tried to drown myself. I'm ashamed of that now. Jack saved me. He was out fishing. He took me home, looked after me, made me tell him about the children, and ever since he's been working to get them back for me, all at his expense.'

'How can he get them back if the police and courts can't?'

'Jack says it's best I don't know. He has many contacts throughout the world. He's employed detectives, paid for everything, given me money, built the pottery, given me a future, and above everything, hope! Soon, he says, I'll see them. Amy, they should be back in England soon. In my eyes, Jack Coverack is a saint. He asks nothing in return and there are many people in Rosemullion and beyond who owe him a great deal.'

Amy sat back, astonished. Quiet, confident Michela, with such a story seething beneath that gentle exterior. And Jack Coverack, too! She'd hardly reckoned him a saint. She felt a sudden rush of happiness for Sue, but what about Ben? There was a connection, and hadn't Ben warned her off Jack? So, if Jack was the saint was Ben the sinner? She gave Michela a hug.

'I'm glad and I hope it's nearly over. I hope I see your children, too.'

'I hope so. I'm sure you will. I feel optimistic at last.'

'One thing,' Amy said. 'Is there any connection between Jack and Ben?'

'Jack and Ben? Why should there be?

The painting group of course, that's all I know. Why?'

'You didn't know Ben before?'

'No. He came in the shop a lot when he was on the course. We became friends and he went out fishing with Jack. I think Mike went, too. Why?'

Amy bit her lip. It would be wonderful to confide in Michela but she daren't risk it. Michela was deeply indebted to Jack and any conversation would surely be reported back to her benefactor. Amy knew she must work it out for herself.

'Nothing. I just wonder sometimes about Ben,' was all she dared venture. 'I think we'd better check that meat. There's a scorchy kind of smell.'

The sausages and drumsticks were rescued just in time. Amy set them on a warm plate and began sluicing out the blackened pan. Suddenly the boat gave a lurch, throwing her to the other side of the galley. At the same time she heard a roaring noise. Michela gasped.

Amy dropped the pan and she and Michela raced up on deck. It was nearly dark and a heavy sea was running, but it was the wash of a larger boat that had caused the violent lurch, a speedboat running ahead of them, a sleek boat with no lights. A swinging turn brought it round to face them.

Amy waved and yelled, but the boat raced towards them.

'Michela, look out, it's going to hit us.'

She leaped to one side, hanging on to the rail. There was a horrible grinding scrape as the yacht swayed perilously down towards the water. As it slowly righted itself Amy saw the other boat speed away. Then there was a lot of noise and shouting as Jack and Ron appeared on deck.

'You all right?'

Jack ran to Michela who was kneeling on the deck.

'Yes, fine. I lost my balance. That boat, it tried to ram us.'

'Nonsense,' Jack said quickly. 'Why

would it do that? We saw it as we were coming back. Some idiots playing games. There's a race on farther south so it's probably some drunken stray that lost its way, wanted to ask directions then took fright when he hit the yacht.'

'We should call the police,' Amy exclaimed, rubbing a bruised shoulder.

'No point, they'll be miles away by now. It was a powerful boat. I'll check for damage in the morning. It can't be much.'

Amy's heart was still racing. Jack put an arm round her.

'You'll feel better after supper. Let's eat, we're starving.'

'So where's the wine?' Michela asked.

'What wine?'

Jack looked puzzled.

'The pub was closed. Sorry,' Ron said swiftly, too swiftly, Amy thought.

'Just as well I found the bottles,' Michela said and took two more glasses from the cupboard. 'How you missed it,

Jack, I'll never know.'

'Just one of life's minor mysteries,' Jack said casually.

More than one, Amy thought, and I'm no nearer solving any of them.

7

The next morning, Amy decided to walk from Gull Cottage to the studio. She needed to clear her head. It had been a bizarre evening. Both she and Michela had been shaken by the minor scrape, as Jack called it, dismissing it. Ron had opened several bottles of the wine and the recollection of the dark shape rushing towards their yacht had grown hazy.

In the light of day, Amy was certain the marauding boat had had a sinister purpose, but also remembered Jack had asked her to come to the studio to talk about the new painting class. She enjoyed the walk through Rosemullion, and tried to forget the odd events of the previous night.

Fewer visitors strolled around the harbour and a cool breeze and hazy sunshine spelled out late summer. The clear, brilliant blue sky and sun-baked Mediterranean feel had vanished. The season was on the turn. Amy knew she'd always feel the pull of the village whatever the season, and that she'd return many times.

The studio looked as familiar as her own home. Jack was by his car and he looked surprised to see her.

'Amy, what brings you here?'

'You must have drunk more wine than I did. Don't you remember? You wanted to see me about the new course.'

'Did I? Well, lots of things happened last night. There's no reason for me to see you about the class. You're much better at it than me. Do what you want, and it's twice the hourly rate! It's an intermediate class this time.'

'No need to go over the top, but OK, I'll take it.'

Amy reminded herself she wasn't in a position to turn down good money.

'Well, that's settled. I've an appointment in Truro, I'll be late.'

'Michela's around?'

'Ah! She's gone away.'

'Away? Where to? She never mentioned it.'

'It was sudden, spur of the moment.'

Jack dangled his keys impatiently, edging towards his car.

'What about the shop?'

'Sally, local school kid. She'll be in later. Perhaps you wouldn't mind, in the meantime.'

He slid into the driving seat.

'Will Michela be away long?'

'Probably not.'

He switched on the engine, and leaned out of the window.

'How's Sue?' he asked.

'All right, as far as I know. I haven't spoken to her since I got back from Devon. There's not been time. Jack, what . . . wait!'

But he was already on the road, leaving her in sole charge until the unknown Sally arrived. In fact, she didn't arrive until mid-morning, after the first wave of tourists had already left.

Amy's final weary thought as she tidied up and left the studio at five o'clock was that Jack Coverack had a nerve swanning off all day and she hoped Sue wouldn't get too involved with him. She was glad to get back to Gull Cottage. She hadn't yet unpacked from Devon, and the fact she was in Ben's room was strangely unsettling, although there were few signs of his presence. She sat on the bed, Ben's bed! Jumping up, she started to hang up her clothes.

A couple of sweaters and a jacket hung in the corner of the fitted wardrobe unit. She remembered Ben wearing one of the sweaters. Putting her shoes on the floor, she noticed a black baseball cap. She picked it up, and put it on a shelf then noticed that the cap had covered a metal lever on the floor.

She gingerly knocked it with her foot and sprang away in surprise as the back wall slid away to reveal a storage space behind. Stooping, she could see a jumble of stuff on the floor, all black.

There was a jog suit, a wet suit, goggles and, as she pushed the false back farther, saw there were shelves holding files and, the biggest surprise of all, a lap-top computer.

She tentatively flipped open a file — photographs, lots of them. The top one was of a smiling, young blonde who was looking up adoringly at Ben, a Ben laughing and incredibly attractive in swimming trunks, the girl barely covered by a scanty bikini. Amy picked it up, turned it over, then dropped it back quickly and shut the file. So that was Lucinda! *Lucinda and Ben, Cornwall's best summer* was scrawled on the back.

The lap top was much more tempting. It was a make she used herself, easy to get into, battery on live. It wouldn't hurt just to take a peek. Maybe there'd be a clue, some answers to questions surrounding Ben.

There was no sound in the cottage. Mike and Morwenna had gone to Plymouth and the other guests were out enjoying the end of the day. She pushed away guilt and activated the processor. She flicked through the files and one leaped out. LUCINDA. Her fingers hovered . . . dare she? Her breath quickened and then froze at the sound of a car outside, a familiar engine sound. Then came a slammed car door. It had to be Ben. No time to look, just bundle everything back in the cupboard. The doors jammed! She tugged at the lever but it wouldn't budge. She heard footsteps on the stairs so she slammed the outer doors of the unit and went out of the room.

'Why, Ben,' she exclaimed as they met almost head on. 'I didn't think you were coming back. Morwenna said . . . '

Ben's own stride checked. Guilt and confusion were written all over Amy's face.

'What are you doing here?' he said more harshly than he intended.

'Er, nothing. I came back early and the only room free was the one you usually use. Morwenna said it'd be all right.'

'I'll talk to Morwenna later.'

He sounded grim.

'I'd be happy to move out. In fact I was just unpacking. I can find somewhere nearer the studio.'

Her voice was odd, breathless, high-pitched. She stood with her back to the door, praying he wouldn't demand to go in for his sweaters. For several seconds he stared at her. She met his gaze, held it, then lowered her eyelids. She should not have looked into his things. She should tell him.

'Ben,' she started.

'It's no matter,' he cut in quickly. 'I'm leaving Rosemullion tomorrow. I don't need the room. I'll take the sweaters I left.'

He made a move to the door.

'No, no, it's a terrible mess in there. Things all over the place.'

'That doesn't matter,' he persisted.

'You said you're leaving?'

She tried to divert his attention. He nodded. Had Morwenna moved his stuff in the cupboard? He needed to get in there to check.

'When will you be back?' Amy asked.

'I won't, not for a while.'

He watched her closely. She was agitated, nervous. Had she already found something? He thought rapidly.

'So, I thought I'd take you out to dinner tonight.'

He had to keep an eye on her for the next few days, check whom she saw, whom she phoned.

'All right.'

Amy didn't hesitate. It would be her last opportunity to find any answers. Then Ben would leave, and it would be over.

'In fact, you could come now,' he said.

'This minute? It's a bit early for dinner.'

'We can go for a walk, have a drink. It's nearly six. I'll wait here for you.'

'No. I need to shower and change. I've been in the studio all day.'

She had to get rid of him. He was too close to coming into the room.

He smiled.

'You look fine, beautiful in fact. Were you with Jack at the studio?'

'Jack? No.'

She felt heat rising from her toes at his throw-away compliment.

'Jack had to go to Truro, and Michela's gone away, too.'

'Has she now?'

Ben looked puzzled.

'What a way to run a business. I can't tempt you out?'

'You can, later. Give me an hour.'

'An hour! Too long. I'll pick you up in half an hour. No argument.'

Amy showered quickly and changed into a swirling full-skirted dark cornflower-blue dress. Strappy white sandals, a short-sleeved white woolly jacket finished off the outfit and the mirror told her she looked good. It was her last night with Ben Peterson. She'd find out more about him if it killed her! The wardrobe was ajar. She'd managed to unjam the inner sliding panel and put everything back as she'd found it, yet she was still sorely tempted to click on to that Lucinda file.

Instinctively she felt there must be a key to the mystery of Lucinda and Chalfrey Manor. The two were certainly connected. It'd only take a second and she still had ten minutes before Ben came. Suddenly a deep laugh floated up to the window. She glanced out and below saw Ben sitting astride the stone wall talking to Mike, his face animated and smiling. He looked up and waved. She turned back and ran out to meet him.

The evening was balmy, untouched as yet by autumn's cooler grasp. They enjoyed a lovely walk in the evening sunshine, and were now about to enjoy their meal. Ben raised his glass and looked into Amy's eyes.

'To Rosemullion,' he said.

'Rosemullion, a magic place.'

'You'll come back?'

'I hope so. It all depends.'

'On what?'

'All sorts of things. What Sue and I do in the future, for instance.'

'Sue and you?'

Amy pressed her lips together. The atmosphere was too beguiling and she wasn't going to reveal her secret dream, not tonight and not to Ben.

'My cousin, I told you. We have a house in Bath together. She came to stay after . . . after the hospital thing.'

Ben leaned towards her and took her hand lying on the table.

'Amy, I have to apologise for that day. I over-reacted. I was worried about you. I thought you were on the beach, or worse, in the sea. The last place I expected to see you was at Chalfrey Manor in an ambulance. What on earth were you doing there?' he added casually.

Amy took a sip of wine to avoid his eyes.

'I was looking for you. You were away so long. I told you, I got lost and fell into that cellar. Does it matter? I wasn't really hurt. No harm done.'

'I suppose not.'

'And, if we're going to talk about it, why did you warn me off Jack Coverack? What do you know about him? Surely you hardly know him, the few times you went to the painting class. Jack's a good man.'

'You've seen a lot of him?'

'I work for him, but no I haven't seen much of him. I told you, I've been away in Devon all last week.'

His grip tightened, his eyes intent, never leaving her face.

'It didn't register. What were you doing in Devon?'

She pulled her hand away.

'I was on business.'

'What sort of business?'

'Personal, private.'

Antagonism, never far beneath the surface, flared, threatening to spoil the evening, until Ben laughed lightly.

'Sorry, none of my business.'

The waiter's appearance defused the tension and they found a common interest in food and wine, the question of choice absorbing them. When the waiter had taken their order and left, Ben touched her lightly on the hand.

'It's our last evening, so let's not argue. Make a pact, no more questions, keep to the present.'

'Right, I'll drink to that. It sounds sensible to me.'

'The trouble is, Amy Barton, when I'm with you I don't feel very sensible.'

It was a challenge, a charged moment, and from then on they both relaxed. They talked books and films, argued opposite tastes in music, and Amy put aside her suspicions and the knowledge that Ben was leaving the next day. She simply enjoyed the moment.

After dinner, they walked hand-in-hand around the harbour, then away from the lights of the village along the cliff path and down to the darkened beach. Amy took off her sandals, ran to the water's edge, and let the moonlit water ripple over her feet.

'It's magic,' she whispered, 'pure magic.'

'It is,' Ben said and took her in his arms.

He kissed her and she kissed him back. The waves covered their feet, receded, came back and snatched at their ankles. Ben's kisses deepened and Amy clung to him knowing that whatever he was, whatever mystery surrounded him, she was lost. Her heart had betrayed her and again she'd probably chosen unwisely. She'd fallen in love with Ben Peterson!

'Ben,' she breathed, 'I . . . '

'Don't.'

His mouth came down on hers again and she surrendered to the magic of his body against hers. But she had to speak.

'Ben.'

'No, don't.'

His voice was hoarse. He tried to stop her, put his hand over her mouth.

'I must. Ben, none of it matters.'

His hand fell away, his arms loosened.

'Amy, don't spoil it. Wait.'

'No, because it doesn't matter really. Whatever you're doing, or have done, I don't care.'

He stepped away and she felt the cold water round her feet, the wet sand between her toes. She shivered as Ben spoke, his voice cold and angry.

'What are you saying?'

'I'm saying that it doesn't matter,' she repeated, passion ebbing swiftly as Ben moved farther away from her. 'What you are — at Chalfrey Manor. I overheard you.'

The explosion of anger was barely controlled.

'So, you were spying on me all the time. You knew, didn't you? You've known all the time and I fell for it, took you straight there. All this seduction was pre-planned.'

He grabbed her wrist and pulled her back to him.

'What are you up to, Amy Barton? Who sent you here?'

Now she was frightened and tried to break free.

'I don't know what you're talking about. Ben, let go, you're hurting me.'

The tide washed round them and a strong wave caught them both off balance. Amy pulled away and started running up the beach.

'Amy,' Ben called after her.

She turned.

'Don't you dare follow me. Just leave me alone.'

'I'll take you home.'

Ben's tone was uncertain. He started to walk towards her.

'No. Don't come near me. I can see myself home.'

She couldn't help the sob in her voice.

'And thank you for a wonderful dinner.'

She ran quickly towards the road, realised she'd dropped her sandals but didn't go back. Once on the road, she ran faster, never feeling the hurt of gravel on her bare feet. The hurt and humiliation in her heart was much more cruel. She'd made an absolute fool of herself, again.

8

Amy ran back to Gull Cottage, anger fuelling her speed. She was angry with Ben but furious with herself. He had taken her out, charmed her, lured her on. He obviously thought she was hiding something and beneath the attention charm, the probing had continued. She realised that now.

She'd foolishly thought he was attracted to her and she'd let her guard down, but not for one second had he let anything slip about himself. Well, too bad. The key to the Ben Peterson mystery was in that lap top and she had no qualms now about using it.

As she inserted the key into the lock, the front door of Gull Cottage swung back and Morwenna stood in the doorway. Her tabby cat sidled swiftly out into the night.

'My dear life, Amy, what's the

134

matter? Didn't Ben bring you back?'

'No ... I didn't ... he wasn't ... sorry, I thought you'd be in bed by now. I've got a headache. See you in the morning.'

She ran up the stairs. Morwenna watched her, then went into the kitchen, reached for the wall phone and punched in Ben's mobile number.

Amy stood with her back to the door, trying to calm her racing pulse with deep breaths before she locked the door and hauled out Ben's lap top from the cupboard. OK, it was spying. So what! Ben's rejection hurt. She called up the files, clicked on LUCINDA, and the screen leaped into life.

Names, charts and dates were all tabulated in some sort of cryptic code. It didn't make much sense and certainly was nothing to do with Lucinda. She must have been on his mind when he named the file. A key pressed at random threw up a computerised map of Europe with what looked like a motorway network. Towns such as

London, Chester and York shot arrows to Europe via Amsterdam and onward to the United States. An enlarged map of South West England showed her own town of Bath, together with Plymouth and routes arrowed through Devon and Cornwall.

Now she was convinced — drug trafficking, and one of the main highways was through Cornwall. Its rugged coastline with so many secluded coves barely accessible by land was ideal. Hauls had been found in the past, small stuff compared with the mega-operation the lap top showed. Run by Ben? She daren't think it. She made herself go on. Numbers next to all the major towns were marked and again it didn't make sense until she looked a second time. The numbers were dates, written backwards and without spacing. Logging went back years so Ben must have been involved in drug smuggling for a long time. She would have wept if she hadn't felt so angry.

She searched on, moving through the

files but none struck a chord until one combination teased her memory. She clicked on and the screen gradually appeared as an attractive picture of Chalfrey Manor, indicating the gardens, grounds, exterior buildings then a ground plan of the entire manor. Diagram after diagram of the whole house followed, moving on to the cellars where of course Uncle Fred's Bunker was marked as such, a small, rectangular room close to the cellar she was sure she recognised as the one she fell into. Next, inevitably, were graphics of Chalfrey Bay's coastline. Then came the final piece of the jigsaw, a list of dates. Scarcely daring to breathe, she pressed the continue key. Then a soft knock made her jump.

'Amy, it's me, Morwenna. Are you all right? You looked upset. Can I come in? I've made you a hot drink.'

Panic made Amy's voice squeak.

'I'm fine, just going to have a shower. If you leave the drink outside I'll have it in bed. Thanks.'

One finger hovered over the quit key in case Morwenna should come in.

'I'm all right, really. Ben and I . . . we just had a . . . well, a silly disagreement. I'm shattered. Good-night Morwenna, see you in the morning.'

There was a pause before footsteps retreated along the landing. Amy went to the door and listened, heard Morwenna bolt the front door, then the rattle of the back door and out to the garden where she and Mike slept in a chalet during the main holiday season.

Amy scanned the dates listed. The last two were starred. She noted that the starred dates were in two days' time. Whatever was scheduled for Chalfrey Manor was imminent. She jotted down dates and file names. Ideally, the information should be printed out but there wasn't printer in the cupboard so she'd have to rely on memory. She was convinced now that Ben was either masterminding a complex and sophisticated drug operation or he was at least a very big cog in a most loathsome wheel. She forced back her personal emotions. She had to do something about it.

But what? Should she confront Ben? Go to the police? But she had no concrete evidence, not unless she hijacked the lap top. It wasn't too late to phone Sue. She dialled the Bath number and waited. At first she'd thought it was Jack who was perhaps straying on the wrong side of the law, what with all his deals and mysterious absences, plus the flash car and the yacht. But it was Ben, not Jack!

The phone kept ringing. Sue must be out and she never remembered to switch on the answer machine. Amy put down the receiver and thought of Jack. He'd know what to do. If he was in, she'd go round now, late though it was. But he was unavailable also. His machine was on so she left a message, asking to see him urgently, first thing in the morning, at the studio. That was all she could do, simply wait until morning.

She never expected to sleep. Her brain was buzzing, her heart bruised, but after an hour's restless tossing and turning, she fell into an uneasy slumber. She was awakened suddenly by a cacophony of sound. Screeching gulls mingled with the insistent ring of the phone.

'Yes?' she muttered.

Still half asleep, she registered the time — seven-thirty.

'Jack Coverack,' the reassuringly familiar West country burr said. 'Your message — what's wrong? Is it Sue?'

His voice was taut with anxiety.

'Sue? Of course not. Why should it be?'

His exclamation of relief hissed in her ear.

'What then? You sounded so panicky.'

'It is serious but it's not Sue. I must see you. Can I come right now?'

'No! I'm going out.'

'You can't.' Amy was equally sharp. 'This is serious. I need your help.'

She paused, as a faraway click told

her someone else was on the line.

'Hello,' she called, 'who's on the line?'

'I am,' Jack said impatiently.

'No, there's someone else.'

There was a softer, barely imperceptible click.

'They've gone. Someone was listening. Jack, you must see me.'

'For goodness' sake, Amy, get a grip. You sound paranoid. Just tell me what this is all about.'

'Not on the phone. Please, Jack, there's no-one else I can go to unless I go to the police.'

'The police! Don't involve them whatever it is. You'll be stuck in the station for hours, believe me. Look, I do have to go out. It's very urgent and I can't put it off. I'll be back as soon as I can. I'll ring you.'

'When?'

'Sometime this afternoon. I promise.'

'Is Michela there?'

'No, Sally's holding the fort. You can give her a hand if you've nothing better to do, then you'll be there when I get back.'

'All right then. Please be as quick as you can.'

'I will, and, Amy, don't call the police, not until you've spoken to me.'

Reluctantly she promised and Jack rang off. For a long time Amy sat on the bed until she heard people stirring and Morwenna clanging frying pans in the kitchen. She had breakfast and forced herself to chat to the other guests about their plans for the day, then watched them leave for the various excursions. It was still only early morning.

'Let me help clear away,' she offered to Morwenna.

'Goodness, no, you're a guest. Haven't you any plans for the day?'

'I'm going up to the studio later. Jack and Michela are both away. I can't think how that business pays.'

'Jack does all right. Excuse me, dear, the phone.'

Amy wandered out into the garden

and sat on the bench by the front door. She could hear Morwenna talking, a blur of words, then her own name could be heard distinctly, then Morwenna's voice dropped to a whisper and she heard no more. When Morwenna came out into the garden she looked faintly uneasy.

'Amy, could you do me a favour? I need some things from the village. Mike's out fishing and the gas people are coming round to check the boiler. They won't say when, just some time this morning, so I daren't go out. Problem is that family party want dinner tonight and I haven't a thing in.'

'Sure, glad of something to do,' Amy replied. 'Just give me a list, or better still, I'll stay here and you get what you need.'

A golden opportunity, she thought, with both Mike and Morwenna out, to check the lap top information and make sure she had the relevant details.

'No, I need to be here,' Morwenna

spoke quickly. 'It's a bit technical, the boiler, I mean.'

'No problem, I'm always happy to walk down to the village.'

Morwenna's list was a complicated affair necessitating much retracing of steps and when it was finally completed, Amy felt she'd earned a coffee. The morning was passing away nicely and as soon as she'd taken the shopping back, she would go to the studio. As she walked up the hill to Gull Cottage, she stopped to rest a moment and drew well to the side of the narrow road to let a couple of cars go by. Bending down to pick up the bags, she didn't notice a third car until it drew alongside.

'Amy.'

At the familiar voice, her stomach churned. Ben leaned across and opened the passenger door.

'Get in,' he commanded.

'What? I wouldn't get in there if you paid me a million pounds.'

'Amy, please, get in,' he repeated. 'I need to talk to you.'

'I don't want to talk to you, and you're causing a traffic jam. I've nothing to say, after last night.'

'You have to trust me.'

Ben ignored the motorists behind him, got out, caught Amy be the wrist.

'I need time. You must understand.'

She wrenched her wrist free and squeezed past the car.

'Just go away and leave me alone. There's nothing to say.'

She started to run up the hill, heavy bags banging against her legs. He couldn't possibly leave his car blocking the traffic. She turned back. Ben's face was dark and he threw her a black look but was forced to get into his car and drive on.

She dumped the shopping on Morwenna's kitchen table.

'Sorry I took so long. I think I'll go straight to the studio now.'

Since she'd seen Ben, all she wanted was to talk to Jack, to share her anxiety and fear.

'That's fine.'

Morwenna avoided her eyes.

'It can be tricky sometimes, village shopping, though I think we should keep them going. Supermarkets'll have a monopoly if we don't.'

Amy left the kitchen and headed for her room. She knew as soon as she opened the door that Ben had been there. She didn't need to check the cupboard. She knew it would be empty, not even a dropped piece of paper. He'd done a very thorough job. The sweaters had gone, too. She ran downstairs. Morwenna was hanging out washing in the garden.

'Has Ben been here, in my room?'

Morwenna paused, peg in hand.

'Why, yes. It was his room. I did tell you. He came to collect the sweaters, and one or two other things.'

She turned away, busying herself with securing flapping sheets.

'Morwenna, please, what else did he take? Do you know?'

Morwenna gave the sheet a sharp shake.

'I don't know and if I did, I couldn't say. Don't interfere, Amy. Just let things be. Maybe it's time you left Rosemullion, before it's too late.'

'Too late? For what? Why is everyone so mysterious? You do know about Ben, don't you?'

'Amy, I can't tell you anything but I say again, dear, I've grown fond of you and I wouldn't want any harm to come to you. Take my advice, steer clear of Jack Coverack, and of Ben. Best you go back to Bath. I can't speak plainer than that.'

Her brown eyes were troubled. She knew very little and didn't want to know, but there was danger in the air and she felt it like she felt the approach of the autumn storm winds well before they were forecast.

Amy looked at her for a long minute, then said quietly, 'Thanks, Morwenna, but I can't do that, not now. It's too late.'

Jack was not at the studio when Amy arrived. Sally, obviously feeling over-worked and underpaid, took Amy's arrival as an opportunity for an extended lunch break. Amy was kept well occupied during the afternoon but at least the steady trickle of tourists, looking for souvenirs and end-of-season bargains, prevented her from too much fretting and brooding. Jack finally arrived late in the afternoon, not looking overly pleased to see Amy.

'Sorry if you've had a long wait,' he said brusquely. 'I couldn't get away and I can't stay long.'

He looked tense and preoccupied, seemed not to care at all what had been happening in the shop and studio.

'You make coffee and something to eat and I'll close down. Get rid of Sally and you can tell me what's bothering you.'

Amy shrugged. He'd be losing valuable evening trade but she'd come to the conclusion long ago that shop and studio were 'way down on Jack Coverack's list of priorities. He had to be running lucrative sidelines elsewhere with the studio complex merely a front.

Half an hour later, Amy had his full, undivided attention as she told him about Chalfrey Manor from what she'd overheard that first time on the picnic with Ben, through to the discovery of the information on the lap top.

'You printed it out?'

It was the first time Jack had spoken.

'No, there was no printer and Ben went back to Gull Cottage. Morwenna got me out of the way deliberately. She must be in on whatever's going on.'

'I doubt that,' Jack said. 'So, you've no actual proof of anything?'

'No, but it must be drugs. There must be a rendezvous scheduled for tomorrow or the next night. We can't let that happen, Jack. Don't you see how suspicious it is? And it all points to Ben.'

The phone rang. Jack frowned.

'Yes?' he said tersely as he picked up the receiver. 'Just a minute.' To Amy he said, 'I'll take this in the studio. Shan't be long.'

He was a long time on the phone and

she heard terse mutterings, his voice raised occasionally but she couldn't make out what he said. When he came back, it was hard to read his expression and he was silent for a while.

'Well,' Amy prompted, 'what should I do? I thought you'd know. I know about Michela. I hope you don't mind. She's so grateful to you. You're a man who can deal with a crisis, she said.'

'Maybe. Well, at least Michela's problem looks near to solution. No, I can't tell you about it yet, except it's got a happy ending at last.'

Abruptly he changed the subject.

'Your cousin, Sue, does she . . . er . . . has she a partner? A love life?'

All she'd told him suddenly seemed of no account. He'd been absorbed whilst she was talking and now, since the phone call, he was unconcerned.

'Sue? What has she to do with it? Jack, I've come to you for help and all you can ask is how's Sue's love life?'

For once Jack was lost for words. He

150

looked almost pleadingly at Amy.

'Well, since I met your cousin, I can't think of anything else. I've been to Bath. I think Sue likes me, but there's something she holds back. I don't know what it is and I need to know. Amy, I've never met anyone like her, so totally honest and straight.'

'She is. She keeps me on the right tracks whenever she can, but I don't think this is the time or place to talk about you and Sue. The vital thing is what am I to do about Chalfrey Manor?'

Jack stared at her. This was a very tricky situation. There was a strong risk of disaster where Chalfrey Manor was concerned. Things were not going according to plan and now Amy's bombshell had to be dealt with. The overriding factor in this particular case was one he'd never had to consider before. This time, a woman was involved, a woman closely connected with the woman he had fallen deeply in love with.

'OK, Amy, I think it's time we called in the police.'

Amy had no possible way of knowing, but Jack Coverack had just embarked on the most dangerous games of his life. She sighed in relief. It was going to be all right. Jack was in charge. When it was all over, she'd be delighted to talk to him about Sue. She owed him that.

9

The flat was quiet. Jack was phoning from the studio. Amy relaxed into the comfortable old sofa, tension draining only to leave a black chasm in the spot where love for Ben had been blossoming so foolishly.

For the umpteenth time, she wondered how she could have been so gullible. Once this was over she'd never trust a man again.

'Ben,' she breathed, 'why did you have to take this route? And why do I have to be the one to make sure you're caught?'

Ben facing trial? Ben in prison? She squeezed her eyes shut. Best not to think about it, best to leave Rosemullion right away. She'd done what she had to do and Jack could sort it out with the police. If she hurried back she could pack her bag and leave Gull

153

Cottage within the hour.

Jack met her at the door.

'Amy, where do you think you're going?'

'Back to the cottage. It's time I left.'

'You can't leave. You've started this and you're going to finish it.'

'Why? It's nothing to do with me now. I've warned you, told you what I found. It's a local affair, nothing to do with me at all.'

'I don't think so. The police will want to talk to you, especially if they make an arrest. You'd need to identify Ben and maybe the caretaker at Chalfrey Manor. Perhaps he's an accomplice.'

'Identify Ben? I couldn't do that. Isn't it enough that I've told you?'

'You did what you thought right,' he said slowly, 'but now you've got to go through with it. I've arranged to meet the police at Chalfrey Manor.'

'When?'

'Tonight. Now. We must go.'

'But tonight's not the date on the file. It's tomorrow or the next night.'

'They want to be sure, and in any case they need to check the area.'

He pulled at her arm. She resisted.

'Why do I have to come? I don't want to see Ben in trouble.'

'He already is in deep trouble. Drug trafficking — thousands of lives wrecked, misery you'd never dream of. You've already made your choice by telling me all this, and you can't let him get away to ruin more poor wretches. Besides, Ben Peterson may only be a minor player. It's the big guys the police want and you could be giving them that chance.'

'OK. I'm sorry, Jack, you're right.'

The night was black, starless, and a chill wind struck cold off the sea. Amy shivered as she got into the car.

'Jack, shouldn't I have rung Morwenna? I came out without my key.'

'Don't worry,' he said. 'I've already done that.'

She looked at him in surprise.

'I didn't want her to call out a search party. I told her you were staying over with Michela at the studio,' he said abruptly.

155

'But Michela's not there. That's a lie.'

'Ah, well.' Jack shrugged. 'What's one lie more amongst all the others?'

'What others? Jack, what are you talking about? What is going on?'

She glanced at him, and suddenly felt a frisson of fear.

As they neared Chalfrey Manor, her sense of unease increased.

'Jack, what's the penalty for wasting police time?' she asked worriedly.

'You'll know soon enough. We're here.'

Jack had slowed the car practically to a walking pace, and with headlights dimmed was driving up the long drive to the manor. She peered into the engulfing darkness.

'There's no sign of any police,' Amy said.

'You didn't expect cars with flashing blue lights and sirens, did you? We'll go round the back. I'll leave the car over there.'

Amy was nervous, reluctant to leave the car. Dimly she made out the dark shape of the Manor, now looking brooding and sinister. Jack leaned across and opened the door.

'Get out,' he whispered. 'I'll park over by that tree then join you.'

She watched as the car glided backwards deeper into the surrounding bushes. Then there was silence. Amy coughed nervously. She took an uncertain step forward as gravel crunched and she saw a pinpoint of light.

'Jack, thank goodness you're . . . '

Her speech tailed into a muffled scream as total darkness descended over her head, stifling her cries. A cord round her throat was drawn almost tight enough to cut off her breath and she heard a voice.

'Don't move, and don't even try to cry out. There's no-one to hear you.'

Her arms were caught, loosely tied behind her back and the cord passed round her waist. She felt a tug.

'Now, move forward slowly, the rope will guide you.'

'Where's Jack? The police?' she

choked out through the thick material.

The answering laugh was chillier than the night air.

'The police? There's no-one here but me, and a few friends. Now move.'

The rope jerked. Amy nearly stumbled but recovered then put one foot cautiously in front of the other. Whatever terrible mess had she got herself into the last thing she'd show was fear. She followed her captor into the darkness with an overwhelming bitterness that Jack Coverack, too, was in the racket, the same as Ben Peterson. The rope jerked her towards the manor and Amy tried to concentrate on getting out of this dangerous situation, on staying alive. The walk seemed endless, a nightmare of silent prods and pulls as night air gave way to a musty indoor smell.

She guessed from the hard stone floors that she was being taken along the manor's underground network of cellars and passageways. Finally the bizarre walk ended and a voice barked in her ear.

'Down those steps. Why did you interfere? Now we're stuck with you.'

She felt a final thrust in her back, a clang as the door shut, the lock clicked, and Amy was sure she was in the very same cellar she'd tumbled into on that first fateful visit to Chalfrey. Her arms were only loosely tied and she wriggled them free and undid the rope round her waist. The cloth hood took longer but at last it came off, though it made little difference to the pitch-black. Cautiously she put out her arms then crouched down — a stone wall on her left, steps below. She was sure it was the same cellar. She remembered that last impression the first time before losing consciousness had been hazy sunlight and air.

Gingerly she felt her way down the steps, eyes fixed on the shadowy gloom. It had to be a way out. There was a door, but relief turned to disappointment as her fingers felt a stout lock which was well rusted through lack of use and there was no key anyway. A window to the right was shuttered. Yet there was something in Amy's brain, some fact she couldn't connect, willing her to concentrate, to think. A key and steps! Her brain clicked. Ben, in the hospital, furious because she'd followed him to the manor, dismissive of her spell in the cellar, had said there was a key near the steps. How could she possibly find it in this pitch-black? She flung up her arms in despair, hit a switch and dim light threw the cellar into relief.

The key was on a hook near the top step. The lap top computer data rolled into her brain. There was a network of passages, Uncle Fred's bunker, a long corridor leading away from the house, arrowed exits. There was an underground way out of here!

She caught her breath. It had to be to the cave on Chalfrey Bay beach, a smugglers' route to the bay and its waiting boats, long forgotten, but now revived by smugglers dealing in a more vicious trade. That's why Ben had gone to Chalfrey in the first place and so had Jack and his confederate from London — all part of the same gang!

She'd played straight into their hands, babbling her warnings to Jack who'd obviously relayed them straight to Ben. But she wouldn't let them get away with it. She wasn't going to stay there, a sitting duck.

The key turned silently and there was no sound in the corridor from the house above. Ben's diagram appeared in her brain — turn left into a windowless, dimly-lit corridor, sloping downwards past a double door, two right turns, down the third, a long way down. She was suddenly aware of a low humming sound, air conditioning, perhaps? Then she passed through swing doors and she couldn't help a gasp of astonishment as massive steel doors blocked her way. It had to be Uncle Fred's nuclear bunker.

She gave the door a push. It yielded. She stepped inside and put her arm up to her eyes against bright, fluorescent lights which were instantly dimmed. In the brief instant of illumination she'd registered a room with a long table full of objects she couldn't make out, rolls of what looked like old parchment, and a man's shape hurtling towards her. With a cry she stepped back and was pinned against the doors by a body which was familiar.

'For goodness' sake, Amy, what on earth are you doing here?'

He was dressed in black — the gear from the wardrobe.

'Ben?' she said fearfully.

For a brief second his hold tightened as he pressed her to him, then he spoke urgently.

'Amy, go, right now, through that end door and don't stop until . . . oh, no, the tide's already running. You might have to swim. Remember it's not far through the cave, to the beach. Get out and run like the wind, away from that beach. Hide if you see anyone.'

'It's too late, Ben. I know what you're up to. The police'll be here soon,' she lied desperately. 'I've told them all about you.'

'Just get out. You've no idea what you're in. Go, go, go. Trust me!'

He pulled her across the room and thrust her through the doors into yet another corridor.

'Just run as you've never run before. Run for your life.'

Then unbelievably he held her for a second and kissed her.

Then the door banged behind her and Amy ran. The plaster walls gave way to stone, then rock that glistened with water. The overhead lights were dimmer, farther apart, until she could barely see her way. Still she ran, until she heard a sound which stopped her — the distant sound of the sea, and water lapping round her feet and rising rapidly.

She walked on until the water reached her waist, still rising, and she began to swim. Not far to the cave, Ben had said. The roof was higher, the walls wider, but could she trust him? Maybe this was a way to finally get rid of her! She spluttered in panic, recovered and swam on. The cave's roof was alarmingly close and already she was knocking her head on craggy bumps. Then suddenly she was out.

She found herself in a vast expanse of dark water, close to the cliff face. Now she had only to turn and swim inland to the beach. She put her head down and began a swift crawl towards the few distant shore lights twinkling ahead. What she didn't see was a swift, silent inflatable dinghy moving towards her, circling her. Suddenly she was hauled out of the water, dragged aboard and dumped heavily on the floor of the dinghy. Two shapes clad in the same black close-fitting suits as Ben's leaned down to her.

'That her?' a man's voice said, monotone, flat, not friendly.

'Sure is,' came a more familiar, West Country burr. 'Amy Barton, you're giving us an awful lot of aggravation. I'm afraid it's time to deal with you.

164

Tonight's too important to have you tossing spanners in the works.'

'Where'll we take her, Jack?'

'My yacht. That way we can make it look like an accident. Sorry, Amy, I didn't mean this to happen. You should have stuck to my art classes.'

The engine roared into life and sped out to Jack's yacht.

10

Jack flung a towel at Amy telling her to dry off and not drip over the yacht's upholstery!

'Hardly worth drying off,' the other man said as he peeled off his wet suit. 'She'll be back in the water soon enough, and this time she won't be able to swim for it.'

Amy recognised the man as Ron from London.

'Get rid of her, now. There's only an hour to the rendezvous time and the boss'll want her gone by then. It's been a madhouse bringing the operation forward a day.'

'Didn't have much choice,' Jack said grimly. 'She would have blown it to the police. I'll deal with her. You do your job, look out for signals.'

Jack turned and shot a malevolent look at Amy.

'Why did you have to interfere? You could've kept out of all this.'

'All what, Jack?' Amy spat back at him. 'Your disgusting drug smuggling? You hypocrite — all that misery you so graphically described when you urged me to betray Ben. You're a despicable, evil man and I'll not let you near Sue. When I tell her . . .'

Jack's laugh was ugly.

'You don't get it, Amy, even now. This isn't a movie, it's real. The likelihood of you seeing your dear cousin again is very remote. We can't afford to let you loose. Your talent for meddling will be the death of you.'

Amy gripped the towel and tried to stop shaking. There was going to be no hero coming to her rescue and Jack Coverack was relishing the rôle of villain. She shuddered. But surely he couldn't be that bad. Sue liked him, Michela idolised him. If only Ron would go on deck maybe she could reason with Jack, do a deal, but Ron was sitting up and looking curiously at her.

'Drugs? What's she on about? We don't do drugs. Far too immoral. Tell her, Jack, tell her our game's much more sophisticated, more cultural.'

'Quiet!' Jack exclaimed.

He pulled her up, holding her in front of him, one hand over her mouth.

'Ron, check out the deck. There's someone up there. Make sure no-one comes down here. We don't want anyone seeing her.'

'Too late.'

Ron sank back in his seat as a heavy, thick-set man clattered down the steps. The man checked when he saw Amy, looked interrogatively from Jack to Ron, then quickly scuttled back up the steps.

'Never saw anyone,' he called over his shoulder.

Ron laughed.

'I know how to pick 'em, don't I? This crew will disappear in Amsterdam and a different set of guys'll do the Atlantic run.'

He got up, picked up a length of rope

and came towards her.

'For heaven's sake, get rid of her now. If you can't stomach it I'll be more than happy to oblige. Fair's fair. You dealt with the other one so I'll take her.'

'Other one?'

Amy blanched as he came nearer.

'Your boyfriend, the one you thought was the bad guy. Ben whatever. Might've scuppered the whole operation if Jack hadn't caught him in the bunker taking pictures of the stuff.'

'Ben?' Amy whispered.

''Fraid so,' Jack said carelessly. 'Ben is, or was, one of the good guys.'

Ron was now tying a rope round her ankles.

'OK. I'll take her now,' Jack said and pulled her roughly. 'Now don't think of yelling for help, Amy. The crew's as good as deaf and blind.'

Effortlessly, he threw Amy over his shoulder and ran up the steps. Once out of earshot on deck, he slewed her round to put his mouth to her ear.

'Sorry, Amy, but I had to be

convincing. Listen, there's not much time and I have to throw you overboard or we're both done for. Ron spotted you in the water before I had a chance to pick you up. I'll cut the ropes but keep your hands and feet together as you go over. The sea's calm, so make for the cave to the left of Chalfrey Beach. Whatever you do, keep away from the main beach and with any luck one of Ben's men'll pick you up. Hold still.'

He set her down by the rail. Amy felt the ropes part and had the presence of mind to grasp the severed bits before he lifted her.

'Good luck and keep your head down. They're armed.'

Amy only managed a half-hearted gurgle before hitting the water. She struck out for a second time towards the shore, swimming as much as possible under water, surfacing only to get her bearings, praying she was heading in the right direction. At one point, looking back, she could see the yacht's lights and then towards the shore answering lights started to blink. It, whatever it was, was starting and there was nothing she could do.

A dull ache, a lethargy, began to spread through her tired body and her limbs slowed as she lifted her head. There were no lights anywhere now. She was aware of the sea taking her in a soft embrace so she didn't feel the cold. Movement was too much effort and with a gesture of surrender she threw her arms in the air and was sucked under. Suddenly something jolted her back and a pulse of energy thrust her upwards. She cannoned into something hard. She pushed it away, kicking and struggling.

'Amy, Amy, it's Ben! Stop fighting me. You're safe! I've got you.'

She closed her eyes, convinced she was dreaming.

'Amy! Keep going! We're nearly there. Don't give up on me, Amy. Amy Barton, I love you!'

Suddenly, the ground was hard and

wet beneath her, sea water pouring from her mouth, Ben, above her, kneeling, fighting to give her life and breath, his own breath, calling her name, then shouting out to figures running across the beach, torches bobbing.

'Here, quickly. Here.'

He gathered Amy in his arms and ran towards the lights.

A sudden shocking roar erupted and the sky turned orange as flames leaped into the dark sky. The watchers on the beach instinctively shielded their eyes against the glare.

'The yacht's gone up!'

'Was the stuff on board?'

'Never mind that, take the stretcher up. The car's on the top. Hurry. The police'll alert the coastguard. We need to get Amy to hospital.'

Wrapped in foil and blankets and strapped to a stretcher, Amy saw the stars bob above her as she was carried up the cliff.

'I'm all right. I don't need hospital

again,' she protested weakly. 'I thought you were dead. Jack, he's on the yacht!'

Ben's hand gripped hers, it's warmth flowing through her like a miracle.

'The yacht's gone, but I'm very much alive. It had to be a put-up job with Jack. I had to keep watching the yacht. Jack's signal was a shout, then I lost you. Amy, you scared me. It could have gone so wrong. Don't talk now. Here's the car and I've alerted the hospital. I'm coming with you and I'm not letting you out of my sight again.'

'Jack? I must know. He saved me, helped me escape.'

'I don't know what happened. Blowing up the yacht wasn't the plan. But rest now. We'll know about Jack soon. The police can clear up the mess. We've done our job.'

Hours later, she awoke in a small, private room. Ben was at her side and the same doctor who'd seen her before was checking heart and pulse rates.

'As before,' he said, 'we'll keep you in until later in the day, then discharge you. It's no worse than exhaustion and mild hypothermia.'

He gave Ben a curious look.

'There's a battery of Press and cameramen camped outside. You're at the heart of quite a dramatic story, I believe.'

Ben groaned.

'I don't want them getting to Amy. Let the police deal with them.'

Amy tried to sit up, but Ben took her hand.

'You're coming with me once you're out of here, and you've got a visitor, from Bath.'

As if on cue, Sue came into the room.

'Sue! What on earth are you doing here?'

Sue hugged her cousin.

'And it's not really for you this time. It's . . .'

'Jack! Oh, I'd forgotten. He's not . . . ?'

Amy daren't utter the word, but Sue's face reassured her.

'Jack's alive. He's here, in intensive care. When he came in he was asking for me so the police came to the flat and I drove down straightaway. Nobody told me you'd be in here, too. What is going on, Amy?'

Ben got up.

'I owe you both an explanation, but coffee first, and food. You look shattered, Sue.'

'I'm just confused. But coffee'd be great, thanks. I'll be scared to let Amy out on her own again.'

'Amy's not on her own,' Ben said quietly, 'not any more. Don't go away.'

'Wow,' Sue exclaimed. 'Did he mean what I think he means?'

'Oh, Sue, I don't know. Everything keeps turning on its head. It was dangerous, too, and I never dreamed Jack might even've been killed. So might I. It all turned very nasty. One thing though, it's not drugs.'

'What then?'

Ben came back into the room.

'Coffee in ten minutes. The place is in over-drive, police and Press fighting for space, even a mobile canteen outside.'

'But why? What's so important?'
Amy was puzzled.

'Maybe the way it all ended, a police raid on Chalfrey Manor, an explosion at sea, all that stuff's high drama — a good news story. And if you and I, Amy, hadn't been so suspicious of each other it wouldn't have ended so publicly and dramatically.'

'I knew you weren't a genuine art student.'

'And I suspected you of working with an international gang of crooks, and feared that you were about to ruin something my company's been working on for months.'

'Your company?'

'Afraid so. Durham International Security Limited. It all started as a small family firm run by my father and uncle. It's like a monster out of control now. I promised myself I'd tie up this last case, then I'd quit.'

'This last case? Chalfrey Manor? Jack?'

Ben nodded.

'It's taken nearly two years of my life and a lot of man hours and grief but we've done it. Durham Securities works mainly on behalf of insurance companies. This last one's all about leaking priceless art treasures out of Britain. A very professional, well-organised gang of thieves has been stripping stately homes of antiques, paintings, jewellery, usually stolen to order. That makes it hard to trace. The stuff just vanished. What we didn't realise was that the gang used a series of safe houses in remote areas all around the country to hide the pieces until they could be shipped overseas. They always seemed one step ahead but this time . . . '

A nurse came in with a loaded trolley.

'Sorry, Mr Peterson, best we can do. It's chaos out there.'

'That looks great. Thanks. We do appreciate it.'

She bustled out and Ben poured the coffee.

'Do go on, Ben,' Amy prompted as

she took the coffee.

'We traced them to Cornwall and Jack's their contact here.'

'Jack? Mixed up with a gang of thieves?' Sue asked, grief-stricken.

'Jack's a maverick. The gang approached him to find them a safe house.'

'Chalfrey?' Amy burst out.

'The obvious choice. Jack's grandfather was gamekeeper there years ago. What they didn't know was that Sir Roy Trevain is an old family friend of mine. We've been monitoring Jack for a long time. He . . . well, he overstretched himself on a couple of deals. He needed the money and they paid well. He's been very foolish, but he's not a criminal. God knows what happened in the boat. Anyway, when you turned up from Bath, Amy, where there had been a couple of major robberies, looking for Jack Coverack, I jumped to the conclusion that you were involved with the gang.'

'Was it your boat that buzzed us out on the bay?'

'Not mine personally, but one of my operators, yes.'

'It gave me a fright, and Michela.'

'I'm sorry, but we had no option.'

'What about the timing on your lap top . . . oops!'

She clapped her hand over her mouth.

'Don't worry, I knew all about that even before Jack phoned me. I'm afraid Morwenna helped me to keep an eye on your movements, and Jack re-arranged the schedule once you'd told him what you found. All the gang came running down to Chalfrey, right into the arms of the police. I'd arranged to meet Jack at Chalfrey and get you out of it but it didn't work quite to plan.'

'And what were you doing in Uncle Fred's bunker?'

'Taking photos of the treasures stacked there for evidence later, and worrying about you imprisoned in that cellar, or so Jack and I thought. We never reckoned on you being taken to the yacht. You realise that he saved your life, no doubt about that.'

'But he'll be charged,' Sue said fearfully.

'He's an accessory to robbery, of course, but once the whole picture's clear I would imagine the law will go very easy on him.'

Sue stood up.

'I must go to him. He asked me to marry him earlier, before it's too late, he said.'

'And?'

'Jack's a survivor, and you'll be the second person to know my answer,' Sue said with a smile.

Amy flopped back on the pillows.

'Well! Dan Warren has a lot to answer for.'

'Dan Warren?' Ben asked as he took her in his arms.

'Dan sent me down here, said Jack Coverack was just the man who might have ideas for my future, mine and Sue's.'

Ben's face was close to hers.

'Then Dan Warren must be invited to our wedding.'

'What?'

'Our wedding. I told you, I love you, and you didn't say no.'

'You didn't ask.'

But Ben had captured her mouth, and it was a long time before he let her go, by which time Amy had no desire to be anywhere Ben wasn't.

'So you will marry me?'

'Yes, I will, if you'll tell me about Lucinda.'

'Lucinda?' He drew back. 'My yacht . . . oh, the girl Lucinda. Lucinda is my very dear, sweet goddaughter. She's all of fifteen, admittedly looks a bit older, and she's also a cousin several times removed.'

'Oh, well, in that case . . .'

Pure happiness welled up in Amy's heart as she reached out to draw Ben back to her.

'I can't wait to marry you.'

'Special licence then,' Ben said, 'because neither can I.'

They sealed their contract in a sweetly passionate embrace and Amy knew her life would never be the same again now Ben Peterson had entered it for ever.

★ ★ ★

Ben and Amy were married a week later in the tiny chapel on the hill above the village. The event attracted a lot of media attention but Morwenna and Mike ring-fenced the chapel with a solid body of villagers, cutting off the intrusive Press and TV cameras from the little world inside the chapel.

Amy's and Sue's families came from the Northern Dales and promised a double celebration in Yorkshire when Jack Coverack was fit to marry Sue. Jack made the ceremony, in a wheel-chair and swathed in bandages. Michela and Sue stood guard on either side, and Michela's two beautiful dark-haired children, back safely with their mother, watched the proceedings.

Dan Warren was one of the first to

congratulate the newly-weds on the chapel steps.

'I don't know whether to laugh or cry,' he told Amy, 'sending you into such danger. I never dreamed . . . '

'Of course you didn't.'

Amy reached up to hug him.

'And look at the happiness it's brought me.'

'Yes, I can see that, but Jack Coverack, I can't believe it still.'

'Jack was incredibly brave.'

Ben put his arm round Amy's shoulders.

'You know he blew up his yacht because Ron and the crew saw him release Amy? They tried to shoot him, and Amy, when she was in the water. Jack set fire to some fuel drums before jumping clear. He's the real hero.'

'He'll be all right?'

Dan looked apprehensively at Jack.

'He looks worse than he is, and with Sue to look after him . . . '

Amy waved to her cousin.

'I must go and talk to Jack,' Dan

went on, 'and let you get on back to Gull Cottage. Do you know I really like this place, Rosemullion? It's got something about it. I feel half inclined to buy a cottage in the area.'

'Dan, Rosemullion is a magic place and we'll always come back here, won't we, Ben?' Amy said.

'I hope so.'

He kissed her.

'But right now I can't wait to leave, to set sail in Lucinda, just the two of us and, Amy, I promise you that wherever we go, Rosemullion magic will always follow us. So let's not stay too long at Gull Cottage. There are too many people and I want you all to myself.'

THE END

We do hope that you have enjoyed
reading this large print book.

Did you know that all of our titles
are available for purchase?

We publish a wide range of high
quality large print books including:
**Romances, Mysteries, Classics
General Fiction
Non Fiction and Westerns**

Special interest titles available in
large print are:
**The Little Oxford Dictionary
Music Book, Song Book
Hymn Book, Service Book**

Also available from us courtesy of
Oxford University Press:
**Young Readers' Dictionary
(large print edition)
Young Readers' Thesaurus
(large print edition)**

For further information or a free
brochure, please contact us at:
**Ulverscroft Large Print Books Ltd.,
The Green, Bradgate Road, Anstey,
Leicester, LE7 7FU, England.
Tel:** (00 44) **0116 236 4325
Fax:** (00 44) **0116 234 0205**